VIVIAN
UNTANGLED

VIVIAN
UNTANGLED

Sarah Hartt-Snowbell

Napoleon Publishing

Toronto, Ontario, Canada

Cover art by Sarah Hartt-Snowbell

Published by Napoleon Publishing
Toronto, Ontario, Canada

Le Conseil des Arts du Canada   The Canada Council
DEPUIS 1957   for the arts   SINCE 1957

Napoleon Publishing acknowledges the support of
the Canada Council for our publishing program

Printed in Canada

10 09 08 07 06   5 4 3 2 1

Library and Archives Canada Cataloguing in Publication

Hartt-Snowbell, Sarah, date-
       Vivian untangled / Sarah Hartt-Snowbell.

ISBN 1-894917-25-1

       I. Title.

PS8565 A6755 V59 2006   jC813'.54   C2006-900041-7

I dedicate this book to Leo,
my husband and friend forever
and
to my kids and grandkids,
who keep my inner child alive

THE OLD SHIPWRECK

My brain was halfway out the window on that Wednesday in December. I watched the snowflakes rise and tumble, lightly coating the trees in the schoolyard. White whirling dots settled in tiny drifts along the window ledge, only to be swept up again by odd puffs of wind. The snowy spirals hypnotized me into a sleepy daze. As the Old Shipwreck went on and on about the Plains of Abraham, her crackly voice seemed to slip into a faraway hush. It probably wasn't even the snow that put me to sleep in the first place. It had to be her voice. It sounded like a motorboat humming away on the other side of a lake somewhere. Her everyday voice is actually like one of those summertime bugs that buzz right through your head like a chainsaw. But like I said, this time it seemed softer...more like a hum. Anyway, some teachers can do that, you know. They can put you right to sleep in the middle of a history lesson.

Chucky poked me awake with his pencil. The eraser end. He once poked me with the point and spent the rest of the afternoon answering to The Elephant. When I swung around to give him a "look", he passed me a note. In a creepy monster-voice he drawled, "It's from Deena-bo-beena." Then his clunky boots did a drum roll on the bottom of my chair. He thinks he's such a hotshot when he does stuff like that. What Chucky needs most is a good floggin'-on-the-noggin.

On our first day back in September, Chucky had got dibs on a desk way at the back of the class. By the end of October, the teachers had all agreed to haul him closer to the front, because he was busy flunking out in everything except gym. If you ask me, that was a bad idea. When a teacher decides to move all the stupid kids up a few seats, where do all the smart ones end up? At the back! So by the time June rolls around, all the smart kids'll be flunking out because they'll be stuck way at the back—practically in the storage closet. The truth is, they should have left Chucky where he was.

I unfolded Deena's note and read:

Vivian,
I'm going to Waverly Gifts after school. Come with me. Shelly can't make it. Adios.
—Dynamic D

Deena and Shelly were best friends, and there was nothing I could do about it. I was always just a tag-along. So even though Deena's note made me feel a bit like yesterday's leftovers, I was still glad she'd asked me to go with her.

I ripped a piece of paper out of my homework book and scribbled a note. I handed it over to Chucky and whispered, "Pass it to Deena."

He snickered. "Pass-a-deena, Cali-forn-eye-yay!"

I tried to hold back, but my laugh ended up as a snort. Mrs. Shevarek froze at the blackboard. She whipped around and pierced me with her eyes as my note dropped to the floor. When I bent to pick it up, she snarled, "Vivian Glayzier! I invite you to come up here and share your little note with the class."

In a second, there was a whole lot of gasping and whispering going on.

I wanted to tell Mrs. Shevarek that Deena had started the whole thing, but decided not to. I couldn't take the chance of spoiling things, in case Deena was planning to dump Shelly—and make *me* her best friend.

The truth is, I don't really have any best friends, because I'm just too plain. I'm plainer than Rhona, who's plainer than Marian, who's plainer than anyone in every Grade Six in the entire city of Montreal! I'm not saying that I'm the "ugly" kind of plain...so don't

3

go thinking that. My face doesn't shatter mirrors or anything. It's just that I'm not as smashingly gorgeous as I'd like to be. I'm not tall like Shelly or petite like Deena. I'm somewhere in the middle. Not too skinny. Not too fat. Just medium—and still flat as a board. What bugs me most is my hair! I wanted blonde or curly hair, but I ended up with a rusty-looking mop that tangles up when I sleep. So you have to believe me if I tell you—I won't be in the try-outs for Miss Pre-Teen Universe of '55. Ha! But never mind that. There's still a bunch of stuff about me that I *do* like. I have exactly eight freckles (and I don't need any more, thank you very much). My eyes are green like cat-eyes, and I can even see in the dark. I used to pray for X-ray vision, but actually, what I'd like most is to be able to see around corners—like a periscope. This might sound a bit weird, but sometimes I wish I had to wear glasses, so I'd be able to clean them with one of those little cloths you get from the eye doctor, the pink ones with zigzag edges. If I had to wear glasses, I'd store them away in a blue alligator-skin case with a gold snap.

Mrs. Shevarek didn't give up. "Well? Don't just sit there like a bump on a log."

I felt my voice tremble like dry leaves in the wind. "The note's really quite boring," I said. "I'm sure the class will lose interest."

Mrs. Shevarek's voice was coated in frost. "Get up

here, Vivian. Get...up...here! What do you think I am...a broken record? record?"

I felt my cheeks get hotter and hotter. "But ...but...my grammar's awful," I said.

She stomped across the floor and cornered me at my desk. Then she pried my fingers open and took the note. "If *you* won't read it—then *I* will," she said, her mouth getting smaller and tighter with each word. As she studied my note, she inhaled a small whistling hurricane. Her eyebrows disappeared under her bangs and her big bulging eyes looked like they were ready to burst right out of her head. "Go to the office, Miss Glayzier. Show this note to Mr. Peale, and don't you dare return to this class without his signature on it."

The office reeked of glue and fluid for the old crank-up copy machine. I don't usually mind those smells very much. As a matter of fact, I really like them. But in that office, especially on that day, they got me feeling pretty sick. The office lady turned from her typewriter. "May I help you?"

I squeezed the folded-up note tightly in my fist. "Yes, Miss Cooper. I'm here to see Mr. Peale."

She gave me that oh-you-poor-kid look and said, "Just have a seat. Mr. Peale is due back in the office very soon."

I hope he forgets to come back, I prayed.

The red second hand did laps around the wall clock.

The minute hand jerked into place each time the second hand hit twelve, for a grand total of twenty-seven minutes. I sat there with my stomach jumping around like a fish on the bottom of the boat while Miss Cooper typed on little blue cards and answered phone calls. I watched her file her nails, drink coffee and fold two origami birds. Then she polished her nails. Smudged them. Polished them again—and again. At that point, the office smelled of glue, copy machine fluid, and enough Maybelline nail polish to put your head in a spin.

Suddenly, a large gray blur appeared through the frosted glass door. My heart and stomach felt like they were trading places. *It's The Elephant. Prepare …to…die.*

THE ELEPHANT
NEVER FORGETS

Mr. Peale has two suits, a dark grey one and a light grey one. By afternoon, his clothes get awfully rumpled, and that would be reason enough to call him "The Elephant". Then one day in the cafeteria, Joey Kaplan from 6B whispered, "Peale is Hebrew for elephant. Pass it on." So everybody fired the message around from one table to the next until the whole cafeteria was buzzing and snickering.

I followed The Elephant into his office. Leather. Cigar. Vitalis hair goop. I'd been there so many times that even blindfolded I'd have known where I was.

He motioned for me to sit in the old wooden armchair facing his desk. "Are you aware, Miss Glayzier, that this is your *third* visit to my office this month?"

"Yes, Mr. Peale."

"And do you recall that twice it was for coming to school late?"

"Y-yes."

"Unfortunately, Miss Glayzier, I never forget these things. Now, before we go on, I'll take this opportunity to remind you again that one more late arrival will mean big trouble for you. Is...that...clear?"

"Yes, Mr. Peale."

"Now, tell me, what brings you here *this* time?"

"I wrote a note."

"You wrote...a note," he said, making it sound like a snappy little poem. He stood in front of his big swivel chair then just let himself plop down into it. His chair squawked like a seagull as he swung himself from side to side. He plunked his elbows on the desk and unfolded his glasses. "May I see your note?"

I handed it to him and prayed for a miracle. *Please make the ink disappear right this second.*

He squinted and brought his eyebrows together as he read. Then he exploded. "This—is a *disgrace!*"

"I know, I know," I said. "I'm awfully sorry. Really. I promise I won't ever..."

"You're to stay out of trouble for the rest of the school year, Miss Glayzier! Do...you...understand?" He sprang forward in his chair, crumpled my note and dropped it into his wastebasket.

I jumped up. "Oh! Mr. Peale. I have to bring the note back to my teacher. Signed."

He fumbled around in the wastebasket to find my crunched-up note, smoothed it out on the desk as well as he could and wrote his initials on it.

At that point, his necktie was sort of hanging off to one side, so I couldn't help but notice how his buttons were struggling to keep the two sides of his shirt together. One sneeze and those buttons would have popped right off and hit the back wall. Even worse, right between the third and fourth buttons, you could actually see the hair on his stomach. Believe me, nobody ever needs to see something like that. Most of the time I don't really mind seeing somebody's gorilla hair...like, maybe on some guy playing soccer on Fletcher's Field or an old geezer goofing around in the "Y" pool. Don't go thinking I'm narrow-minded or anything, because I'm just as curious as the next kid about teachers and principals. Sure, I wouldn't mind knowing more stuff about them...like where they live, if they have kids, or even what they do on the weekends. But nobody ever needs to know that the school principal has a hairy stomach. The whole thing's just too disgusting, so don't even get me started on that.

I dreaded going back to my class, embarrassed to death that Mrs. Shevarek and The Elephant had actually read my horrible note.

The janitor was at the far end of the hall, near the library. He had just started up the big twirly-brush machine for waxing the floors. I stepped carefully along the tiles leading to my classroom. *White tiles only—no stepping on the cracks.* I stopped at my locker, unfolded my note and read:

Yes, Deena. I'll go with you to Waverly Gifts. I hate this blasted history class and can't wait till it's over! That creepy old Shipwreck-Shevarek bores me to death. Her dress is ugly with a capital "U" and right this second she has gooey white spit stuck in the corner of her mouth. Yuck!
    -VVN

The classroom door was open. Everyone was gone—everyone, except Mrs. Shevarek.

I handed her my note. "I'm sorry, Mrs. Shevarek. I'm very sorry about this."

"You may leave now," she said, turning to clean the blackboard. I watched the jelly of her upper arm flap and jiggle as she washed away her history notes and the remainder of Mr. Byers' math equations. Still facing the blackboard, she said, "I certainly hope you feel remorse, Vivian."

I zipped up my jacket and stacked my books. "I do feel morose," I said.

The damp cloth stopped making circles on the blackboard. Mrs. Shevarek turned to face me and practically squeaked—"Morose?"

The classroom door clicked shut behind me. What a numbskull! I knew I'd have to look up "morose" in the dictionary as soon as I got home. Morose. I was sure that's what she'd said, but if it wasn't, I had to know what it meant—in case it was something stupid or rude. Even so, it was too late to do anything about it.

I always look up stuff in the dictionary, even though most of the time I end up forgetting what the meanings are. I forget because as soon as I get the dictionary down off the shelf, the whole deal ends up like a snowball rolling down a hill. Like the day I looked up the word "phobia". (I don't even remember why I had to look that one up.) First off, I couldn't find it in the Fs, so I checked for it in the Phs. I admit that I'm no great shakes in school and all, but I'm smart enough to figure out stuff like that. The dictionary said "phobia" meant "an illogical fear". So then I had to look up "illogical". The dictionary showed the meaning as "devoid of logic". So naturally, I had to flip back to the Ds. By the time I finished, getting dragged from one page to another, my brain was so bunged up, I could hardly remember what word I was looking up in the first place.

I flew past the lockers, down the stairs and out of the school. Then I tore out of the schoolyard like lightning and headed toward the gift shop. *Please, let Deena not be angry with me.*

I was completely out of breath by the time I reached Waverly Gifts. Four blocks is usually no problem, but when I run in the cold, my asthma kicks in, and my lungs feel like they're ready to burst. When I pulled the door open, a warm blast from the heating vent tried to melt away my day's troubles. But the day wasn't over—and my biggest troubles were yet to come.

MATH PROBLEMS

The wind chimes clinked out a hollow fading song. As I passed the display of homemade candles and fake flowers, I got a good whiff of cinnamon, strawberry and eucalyptus. Right across from the greeting card counter, I saw her. She was examining a letter opener. "Expecting mail?" I said.

"Vivi! Am I glad to see *you!* Did you get in trouble?" she asked in a voice that seemed a bit too cheerful.

I told her what had happened, and she began to laugh. When Deena laughs, it spreads around like the flu. In a second, she had me laughing too. Not just regular laughing, but the kind that makes you pound your fists into your knees. The kind that comes with tears.

The saleslady came out from behind the cash register and gave us the once-over. She twisted her mouth into a crooked wave and looked up into her eyelids.

When we finally stopped laughing, Deena showed me a brass letter-opener. "How does this grab you?" she said.

"I guess it's okay. You gettin' it?"

"It sure would make a nifty birthday present for my grandfather," she said as she placed it back with the others. "Let's come back for it tomorrow after school. Okay?"

"Why tomorrow?"

"Because it's three-and-a-half bucks, you goof, and I don't have enough on me. That's why."

"Well then, I'll come back with you," I said. "You can count on it."

We hung around outside for a bit and watched a lady drape tinsel on the Christmas tree in the window. Under the tree, in the glow of tiny coloured lights, I saw a white leather diary. The pages were edged in gold. A strap from the back cover wrapped over the front of the pages and slipped into a gold lock on the front cover. Tied to the strap, with fine red ribbon, was a tiny golden key.

"Oh-h-h, Deena," I said. "Just feast your eyes on that."

"What? Where?"

"The diary. Right down there...beside the manicure set...see? Isn't it absolutely stunning?"

"Oh, please!" she said. "It's only a diary, you hangnail. What's the big deal?"

"It's perfectly gorgeous!" I said. "Did *you* ever have a diary?"

"Of course, you doofus! I just got my new one for '55. You?"

I didn't answer.

"Yeah, sure. You probably never even had one," she sneered, then almost screamed, "How can you *live* without a diary? *Everybody* has a diary!"

"Well...my other one's filling up real fast," I said. "When we come back tomorrow, this diary will be mine."

I always wanted a *real* diary, but had to make do with an old notebook I had left over from Grade Four. Besides, Mom always says, "If you ask me, those fancy-shmancy diaries are nothing but a waste of money and a bunch of foolishness."

Deena and I went through our usual string of goodbyes, au revoirs and see-ya-laters. "Snow at last!" she said. "Remember—the mountain on Sunday." As she reached the corner, she called, "And don't forget...the hot chocolate's on *you.*"

I squashed my forehead against the window of Waverly Gifts to take another peek at the diary, then raced home. Great wet snowflakes melted on my cheeks and clung to my hair and eyebrows. The streetlights had come on. I didn't see it happen. I never do. The glow of streetlights just seems to creep up on you when you're not looking. I hurried along, stopping now and then to kick at some of the slush-cruds hanging from the car fenders at the curb. It was awfully late, and I knew Mom would be downright mad if I didn't come up with a pretty good excuse.

Our house isn't really a house. It's called a flat. The Kingsleys live in the bottom flat. They're lucky, because in the summer they can plant a garden, and in the winter they don't have to bust their backs shovelling stairs—because they don't have any. Ha!

The middle flat, where the Gravelle family lives, has at least a dozen outside stairs and, of course, no garden. If you ask me, the Gravelles don't have it so easy, because they have to put up with noise from their upstairs neighbours (for example, *moi!*), and if they make noise themselves, they get complaints from the Kingsleys under them. Mom says that Mrs. Kingsley has dug hundreds of little dents in her ceiling by bashing it with the handle of her broom. She does that every time Jeanine Gravelle practices the piano over her head. The truth is...I *always* hear Jeanine playing her boogie-woogie music. The beat comes right up through the floor of my room—and I love it.

We live in the top flat. That means we get to share the outside staircase with the Gravelles, but once we open the door at the top of the stairs, we end up with a long inside staircase to climb as well. Believe me, it's awful when you have to drag home a stack of books or other heavy junk of one kind or another.

Mom says she dreams of living in a bottom flat so she won't have to go lugging groceries up two flights all the time. But Dad complains that a higher rent would break him altogether. "Even *fifty* a month for this dump is highway robbery," he says.

Nobody had bothered doing any shovelling yet, so I scraped my boots back and forth through the snow on each step to clear my own pathway up to the outside door.

Mom swung the inside door open. "Where on earth were you?" she said in her most frantic voice. She was holding a knife.

I slipped by her, dropped my schoolbag onto the little hall table and shimmied out of my jacket. "I was delayed," I said, following her into the kitchen.

"What do you mean 'delayed'?"

I watched her cut the ends off the last few string beans and dump them into the enamel pot on the stove. "I was delayed by Mr. Peale," I said.

"Whatever for?"

"He was commenting on my writing."

"Oh! You must tell us all about it at suppertime. But right now, you'd better get started on your homework."

I closed my door and flung my books onto the bed. Homework, nothing! First things first!

I made a list of all the most likely places to find money, did a careful search, and filled in the amounts.

Square wooden bank   13 ¢

Schoolbag   9 ¢

Junk drawer   3 ¢

Desk drawer   4 ¢

Night table   0 ¢

Window ledge   5 ¢

Under the bed   0 ¢

Bottom of the laundry bag   12 ¢

Pockets of everything I own   12 ¢

A grand total of fifty-eight cents!

Math Problem:

Vivian needs a white leather diary with gold all around the edges. The cost of the diary is $3.79. After doing a thorough search of her entire room, she found a measly 58¢.

1. How much more money does Vivian need to buy the diary?

2. What's the best way for Vivian to get the money she needs?

My life is no picnic. Deena, the most popular kid in the whole school, had a bicycle all her life, and white furniture, and a backyard with grass. Then there's Shelly. Cool Shelly with her perfectly ironed blouses that stay tucked in and pure white bobby socks that always stay up. I'm the one stuck with ugly hand-me-downs—second-hand clothes from people I don't even know. I'm the one with torn-at-the-toes socks that creep their way down into my scuffed-up Oxfords. Every time I ever need anything, Mom says, "I hope you understand, dear, but you'll just have to wait for a good payday." Then payday comes along, and so does the phone bill or a brake job for the old Studebaker. Dad's car is older than I am, and it has rust all around the edges. He just laughs and calls it his lace-trimmed chariot. On days when Dad gives me a lift in the morning, I ask him to drop me off a block away from school. "The walk is good for my lungs," I tell him, and he believes me. He doesn't know that I'd rather die than have any of the other kids see me getting out of his rusted-out jalopy.

The sound of Dad's car spluttering to a stop at the curb and the smell of corn and string beans told me it was suppertime. I dropped the fifty-eight cents into my pencil box and spread a few open books out on my desk so that any snoopers would think I was really up to my eyeballs in homework.

Dad stabbed his fork into a jumble of string beans. "So, Vivi. How was your day?"

"I've run into a problem," I said. "Sort of a math problem."

"Remind me after supper. I'll help you work it out before driving you over to Grandpa's."

Mom poured water into our glasses. "Dan," she said,

"have you been getting any new business lately? Anything from Silhouette? How about Paisley? Did they place any orders?"

Dad clinked his fork onto his plate. "Aaaah, I wish, Jenny," he said. "They haven't given us any business for months, and that old galoot Henderson says nobody's getting a raise this year. He says with business the way it is, we're all lucky to have jobs...and we'd better not make waves. Imagine."

"Oh, darn!" Mom said. "Isn't there anything you can do about it?"

His voice flew up a whole notch. "Don't be such a worrywart!" he said. "We have to take it one step at a time, and that means cutting corners."

"Cut corners! Cut corners!" shouted Mom. "That's all we ever seem to do!"

Dad pounded his fist on the table. He almost had all the forks and knives jumping right off the plates. "We're not the only ones, for cryin' out loud!" he shouted. "And in case you haven't noticed, *everyone* has money troubles these days! That's reality...don't you get it?"

I'm not an absolute dimwit, you know. That's probably why people are surprised that I don't do so great in school. Even my teachers don't know that when it comes to solving everyday problems, I'm no slouch. Not that I can figure out square roots or breeze through long division like some kind of Einstein. No. It's that

I'm pretty good at things that really matter. Like, at carnivals, I can usually come up with a pretty close guess about how many beans there are in a jar. Okay, maybe that's not the best example. Once, right in the middle of Woolworth's, a whole bunch of people kept trying to get this baby to stop crying. "Maybe he's thirsty." "Maybe he's wet." "Try picking him up." They carried on as if they'd all just graduated from Doctor Spock University. After they all gave up, I figured I'd give it my best shot. A few peek-a-boos—a couple of funny faces—and, within seconds, the little guy turned all cute and giggly. That's the kind of stuff I mean. I'm pretty good at things like that. So what I'm getting at is that, lots of times, if I really put my mind to it, I can even get my parents to snap out of their crummy moods. Don't get me wrong. It doesn't work every time, but just on the odd chance that it might, I'm always ready to give it a try.

"Say, here's a good one," I said. "A big moron and a little moron were walking along the edge of a cliff. The big moron fell off. Why didn't the little one?"

Mom yanked off her apron. She kept firing words at Dad as if she hadn't even heard me. "That Drapeau and his promises!" she continued. "Little shrimp of a mayor...he's leading us all into the poorhouse!"

Dad's voice boomed, "Give the man a chance, for heaven's sake! He's only been in office a few months, and if I remember correctly, *you* voted for him."

"He was a little more-on," I said. "Get it? He didn't fall off, because he was a little...more...on."

Mom gave me a look. "Please! This is no time for your foolishness!"

It seemed that neither one of them was in the mood to switch to another mood.

Dad shoved his chair back hard enough to chip the paint off the wall. "There's no point in rehashing our budget right this second," he roared. "The whole thing can wait till later...when we're alone. So just drop it!"

Well, isn't that just dandy! Now they've got themselves caught up in a math problem all their own, and it looks like mine's gonna have to wait.

FIX-IT NIGHT AT GRANDPA'S

Grandpa says that girls are usually cheated out of learning important stuff. He says that everybody should learn how to splice electric wires, refinish furniture and solder pipes. So on my Wednesday visits to Grandpa's, we usually fix things...or make things. Grandpa always says, "If y' have only one hour to do a task, you'd be wise to spend the first forty-five minutes planning and measuring. If y' do that, then the rest of the job will be as easy as pie."

We've built birdhouses and knick-knack shelves. We wired up a lamp and installed two light switches. I even helped him change a few worn-out washers to stop the taps from dripping. Grandpa promised that he'd even let me help him do some plastering and painting in the spring. "You're ready for life," Grandpa says. Whenever we finish a job, he hugs me and says that. "You're ready for life." I love when he says that.

Of course, my visits to Grandpa's are not only

work-work-work. We always set aside time for a few games of chess. When I was a little kid, maybe five or six, he taught me the names of all the pieces, how each one moves, and how to plan my strategy. Now I even beat him sometimes.

The worst thing about Grandpa is that his place is one gigantic mess. It's even worse than *our* place. He keeps boxes of things everywhere. Broken watches, cameras, radio parts and all kinds of electrical stuff. He has stacks and stacks of newspapers and magazines. He says there's a few articles in them that he'll get around to reading one day. (Ha!) Grandpa has two or three vacuum cleaners, all in pieces, in a corner of the dining room. "I hate to throw 'em out," he says. "The minute I throw 'em out...that's when I'll need the parts for somethin' else."

I kicked off my boots and slung my jacket over the nearest doorknob. "I'll drop by around ten thirty to pick you up," said Dad. He tweaked my nose, gave Grandpa's shoulder one of those gentle love-pokes, and left.

"Okay, Vivi. The board's all set up," said Grandpa. "But first, we've got some important fixin' to do. Ready to tear into some tile work?"

I followed him into the kitchen. "Tile work?"

"Y' bet yer boots! A few tiles popped up beside the bathtub. Just loosened up, they did, and I can sure use your help. I'll just guzzle down another cup of tea and then we can get straight to work. Need somethin' to wet yer whistle, Vivi? How about a hot chocolate?"

"No thanks, Grandpa. Maybe later on."

He reached for the little brown teapot and filled the granny-cup. That's what *I* always call it. The delicate china teacup had been Grandma's favourite, but after she passed away, Grandpa stashed his own chipped mug way up on the highest shelf. He'd decided to keep Grandma's cup and saucer for himself.

Grandpa dropped three sugar cubes into the strong, dark tea. I watched him chase the cubes around with a little silver spoon to make them dissolve faster than they'd planned. Then he sipped his tea. Slurped it, that's what he did. Grandpa's really a gentleman, but he does slurp his tea, and when I'm with him, I slurp too. Mostly hot chocolate. He never hassles me for slurping, and I never hassle him. It's just something we do.

Grandpa tapped each tile lightly with the back of a putty knife. "See, Vivi. This is how we'll figure out which ones are the troublemakers. It's good to learn about working with tiles, 'cause y' never know when it'll come in handy."

We worked side by side, pulling out the wobbly tiles, clearing away the damp grout and scraping off the old cement.

"Grandpa, I've...I've run into a problem," I said.

"What is it?"

"It's...it's...I can't get the grout out of this corner."

"Here. Try using the small chisel," he said.

I tapped the small chisel straight down with the hammer. The grout came away perfectly, without loosening up any of the nearby tiles.

"Seems like the floor's still a bit damp," said Grandpa. "We'll have to dry it all out before we start to set the tiles back in. But first, take this brush and try to sweep out all those loose particles."

"Grandpa?"

"Yes, Chipmunk. What is it?"

"There's something I have to tell you."

"Okay, shoot."

"I...I sure like doing fix-it stuff with you."

He put his arm around me and said, "You're my favourite fix-it buddy. Did you know that?"

I wanted with all my heart to tell Grandpa about my problem, but every time I tried to tell him, the words got stuck way at the back of my throat. For one thing, I didn't want him to find out that I know zippola about saving money.

Grandpa carefully leaned the tiles against the side of the tub. "You'll find one of those new-fangled clip-on lamps in the dining room. Probably on the shelf beside the window. We can use the lamp's heat to dry all this out before goin' on to the next step. Get the picture, Miss Fix-It?"

"Sure do," I said. "I'll go get it."

The shelf was jammed with stuff. A stack of old phone books with curly pages, April's *Collier's* magazine—all about life on Mars—a seashell collection, and plenty of dust. But no clip-on lamp. "It's not here," I shouted.

He called back. "Go ahead then. Try the china cabinet."

"Okay, Grandpa." I opened the glass door of the china cabinet. What a jumble of stuff! There was an ashtray full of fishing lures, with dust clinging to their once brightly coloured feathers. Off to the side, I saw a sad-looking old radio with all its knobs missing, a sprinkling of dominos that had tumbled from a broken box and a few old prayer books. *Ha*, I thought. *This ain't no regular mess. This is a holy mess!* On top of one of the prayer books, I saw a gold fountain pen and a silver bookmark that had gone all black from sitting around too long.

Grandpa shouted, "Hey! What's takin' so long? Y' buildin' the lamp from scratch?"

"I can't find it," I called.

"Dang! I'll go check the front parlour," he said. That's what Grandpa calls his living room. I'll bet his mom and dad must have called it that too.

While Grandpa was in the front parlour, looking for the lamp, I went back to the china cabinet to take a better look at the gold pen. I picked it up and took off the cap. Then I replaced the cap and set the pen back on the shelf. I began to walk away...but slowly turned back. *What the heck am I doing?* I picked up Grandpa's gold pen once more, hesitated a bit, and then slipped it into the pocket of my dungarees. He won't miss it. *He probably didn't even know that it was sitting there in his holy-mess-cabinet.*

"Aha! Found it," he called from the front parlor. "C'mon and see what we're gonna do now." He stepped into the dining room, and by then it was too late to put the pen back.

Grandpa clipped the lamp onto the bathroom counter, plugged the cord into the outlet over the mirror, and aimed the light toward the floor beside the bathtub. "That should give off enough heat to dry it all out. Think it'll work?"

My hand trembled as I covered my pocket. "Yes," I said. "I suppose so."

Grandpa twirled around, threw his hands up into the air and laughed. "Well, what are we waiting for? While the lamp does its work, we can squeeze in a game or two of chess."

I could hardly look at Grandpa. "I don't feel like playing chess," I said.

"What? No chess? You must be kidding. You *are* kidding, aren't you?"

"I...well, I just don't feel like playing chess right now."

The gold pen felt like lead in my pocket. Red-hot lead burning a hole right through me. My mouth went dry, and my face was on fire with shame. And if that wasn't bad enough, I began to think the most horrible thoughts—*Grandpa's really old. Silver hair and wrinkles. Sooner or later he might get real sick or...or...or maybe even lose his marbles. Then the gold pen won't really matter at all...and he'll probably never even miss it.*

Dad Springs the News

The wipers thwacked back and forth, pushing the snow off to the sides and dragging muddy streaks along the windshield. Dad turned the radio dial to country and western.

Whenever Mom's in the car, she switches the dial away from Dad's favourite station. "I'm sick and tired of all those drunken old cowboys warbling through their noses," she'd say. "Especially that skinny oddball string o' misery."

Dad's absolute favourite singer was Hank Williams. It was a year ago on New Year's that Hank Williams had died, and when Dad had heard about it, he'd just sat around and stared at the floor all day. Some Happy New Year that was!

Flashes of bright neon blues, greens and reds darted into the car as we drove along Main Street. Familiar neighbourhood signs slipped by. Figgler's Deli. Tremblay Hardware. Hogan's Bowling & Billiards.

We listened to Webb Pierce sing the jailhouse song.

Then, as usual, Dad tried to yodel along with Kenny Roberts.

"You're awfully quiet tonight," said Dad, turning the volume way down. "Is everything okay?"

"Yeah."

"Why so quiet, then? Did you lose all the games?"

"Nope. We never even played."

"Well, that's not like you at all, Viv. Did you help Grandpa with any big fix-it projects?"

"Tiles."

Dad's face lit up. "No kidding... Tiles?"

"Yes."

"Hey...what's gotten into you anyway? Doesn't sound like you're up for much discussion," said Dad.

I wanted to stop thinking about Grandpa's pen, but every time I promised myself that I wouldn't think about it, it made me think about it even more.

"What the heck's going on, Vivian? Are you sure there's nothing sitting heavy on your mind?"

"No. I—I mean yes."

"You know, if you ever have troubles, I'm always willing to listen."

How can I tell him I just stole Grandpa's pen? I'd rather die.

I didn't want the conversation to seem one-sided. "How did the budget go?" I asked.

Dad looked startled. "You needn't worry about

those things," he snapped. "It's a grown-up matter."

Home at last. I hit the kitchen first and guzzled down a glass of water. It wasn't even cold, but it was wet enough to fix my dry throat for a while.

Mom was in the living room, poking her crochet hook in and out of her ever-growing afghan. *My mom, The Crochet Machine.* I watched the hook fly up to grab the pearl gray yarn then dive back into the afghan. Over and over. I could tell, just by looking at her, that they'd had one of their big fights about money again. I bent to kiss her cheek. "G'night, Mom."

"Good night, Vivian. Sleep well," she said.

I was sure that she could see right through my pocket. I reached in, gripped the pen tightly and walked slowly to my room.

I flung my clothes onto the chair near the window and put on my pyjamas. On the way to the bathroom, I sneaked Grandpa's pen along under my towel. I squooshed a bit of toothpaste onto my finger, rubbed the pen with it and polished it with a corner of the towel. Wow! Good as new. Polished it again, just to be sure, and once more for good luck. *I will not think about it any more...and that's a promise.*

Mom tapped on the bathroom door. "What's taking so long in there?"

"I'll only be a minute, Mom."

Back in my room, I dumped an old chain necklace out of its thin blue box. In its place, I set the shiny gold pen that I'd neatly wrapped in two layers of Kleenex.

"Heavenly Father," I prayed. "I know You saw me take Grandpa's pen. I'm really, truly, awfully sorry. I'm not a bad person, You know...and I do hope You believe me. If I ever needed forgiving, it's right now."

I searched the folds of my quilt to find my ragged old bear. "Theodore, my oldest and best friend of all time. Just on the odd chance you have the power to know what's going on, I hope you forgive me too."

I turned off the bedside lamp. Wrapped in darkness, I listened to the familiar sounds of night— the fridge motor kicking in and out, the hum of traffic and the drowsy moan of a distant train. Dad's voice drifted in from the hallway. "My decision is final! *Nothing* will make me change my mind," he said. "I'm leaving. *Leaving!* You hear me? I just can't take it any more."

DEVIL OR ANGEL?

Even though he stood a bit slumped, the king was at least a fingernail taller than the frowning bishop. One of the scrawny white pawns inched its way through the gloomy mist and poked the king with the nib of a gold pen. "Aha!" said the pawn. "My pen is mightier than your sword." The pawn jabbed the king over and over. "Take that! And that!" The king buried his face in his hands. His tears spilled through his fingers and splattered at his feet. A salt-water flood spread across the board.

"Pull yourself together," his men scolded. "And if you have to cry, for Pete's sake, limit yourself to the white squares. It's strictly forbidden to cry on the black squares."

The king gazed at the queen, who had been dropped, feet up, into a plain wooden box. Her crown was bent out of shape, and her face seemed frozen in shock. He bowed his head and clasped his hands together. "My beautiful queen. My Rosie."

The pawn began to cry: "I'm blocked. I can't move any more. I just can't."

"Move! Move!" the knights roared, but the pawn was stuck to its square.

The early morning sparrows twittered their way into my dream. I untangled myself from the quilt and tucked Theodore's fuzzy head under my chin. I studied the irregular bumps and cracks in the ceiling then tried to find all the creepy faces that hide in the lilacs of my wallpaper.

There must be at least five other people in the whole world...maybe even ten or twenty...who have the very same wallpaper as I do. Of all of them, there must be a few who discovered the faces hiding in the lilacs. And there has to be at least one other person wondering if there's another person in the whole world wondering if there's anyone looking at those creepy faces right this second.

I thought about last night's screaming match. I knew it wasn't a dream when I heard Dad say he was leaving. They'd had their share of arguments all right, but I never knew how bad things really were until last night. *Don't let Dad leave,* I prayed. *Please keep my family together.*

*   *   *

35

Gerald and Julian snuck up behind me in the schoolyard and stuffed snow inside the back of my jacket. I just stood there. They did it again, and I laughed. The snow melted and soaked right through to my skin. The whole thing wasn't very funny, but I laughed again.

"Boys will be boys, dear. If you show them that it bothers you, they'll keep on tormenting you." That's what Grandma Rosie once told me. Well, she was wrong. Pretending it doesn't bother me doesn't work at all. The only way to get people to stop shoving snow down your back is to kick their teeth right down their throats.

Gerald tripped me, and in a split second Julian helped him push my face into the snow.

A voice from nowhere. "Hey! Stop it!" It was Mrs. Shevarek. She helped me up. "Are you okay, Vivian?"

"Yes, I'm fine, Mrs. Shevarek." I couldn't believe The Shipwreck had actually saved me from dumb old Gerald and Julian, especially after yesterday's note. "Thank you for saving my life," I said.

Deena broke away from a group of kids near the fence and ran to me. I tried to act calm, but the words just tumbled out. "My parents are splitting up. My dad's leaving." I tried very hard to hold back, but the tears started just the same.

"Oh, no!" said Deena. "This can't really be happening. Do you think they might change their minds? Maybe they will, Viv."

"Oh sure! Like parents *ever* change their minds!"

Deena put her arm around me. "This is awful, Viv. It's the worst news you could ever spring on me. You'd better fill me in at lunchtime, okay? Or on the way to Waverly Gifts after school."

I dried my tears on my jacket sleeve. "Listen, Deena, we probably won't even have to go to Waverly Gifts after all."

"Says who?" she said. "I've got to buy my grandfather a present before the weekend rolls around."

I undid the buckles of my schoolbag. "Good. I can save you the trip. Right here, in my schoolbag, I have the greatest gift for any grandfather." I pulled out the thin blue box, opened it and unwrapped the pen.

Deena took it from me and removed the cap. She turned it around this way and that. "Oh, Vivi, this is perfect...absolutely perfect!"

"I knew you'd like it, Deena. It's yours if you want it."

"You sure? I know my grandfather would simply flip over it!"

"Sure I'm sure. For only five bucks, it's yours, Deena. No tax.

I folded Deena's crinkled five-dollar bill in half and then in half again and again until all I could see was half a wrinkly old King George staring back at me. I tucked the fiver into the side pocket of my schoolbag with my pencil box. *Five dollars and fifty-eight cents.*

More than enough for the diary. Even after the tax, I'll have a ton of money left over.

Through the window in the schoolyard, I could see the big round clock in the gym. Eight twenty-seven. With more than a half-hour until the bell, I knew I could make it to Waverly Gifts and back. A bunch of kids gawked at me as I zoomed toward the schoolyard gate. "Back soon, ba-boon," I yelled and began to run. My lungs were screaming for air, but I kept on going.

At Waverly Gifts, there was a sign hanging in the window. "Closed/Fermé". A smaller sign beside it listed the opening and closing times. Opening time: nine o'clock. In my heart, I screamed. NINE O'CLOCK!

Grandma once told me this: "Everybody has a little angel on one shoulder and a little devil on the other shoulder. The little angel encourages you to do only good deeds, but the little devil tries to sweet-talk you into doing only evil."

At that moment, it seemed that they were really there, jumping around on my shoulders—and I got all mixed up in what was probably one of their biggest battles.

It was the angel's voice I heard first. "Quick. Run back to school, Vivian. If you start running now, you'll make it on time for your class."

I turned to run back to school.

The devil's voice blared. "Don't be a dumb

doorknob. They open in a few minutes, so you may as well hang around."

I turned.

The angel pleaded. "You still have time to make it back to school. Run, Vivian. Run!"

I began to run back toward the school.

Then you-know-who with the horns and red tail stamped his foot. "Don't listen to that little twerp," he said. "Turn back now! Don't you want the diary?"

Yesssss! I turned back just in time to see the Waverly Gifts lady twisting the key in the lock.

The devil won the battle.

"Bonjour," said the lady.

I followed her into the store. On the wall behind the counter, a tiny painted bird sprang through the door on the clock and cuckooed nine times. Then, a couple of little wooden people danced in a circle as the clock's music box plinked out a tune.

I could have been in science class. I could have been at my desk like everybody else... But NO! I'm a trouble-magnet, that's what I am.

The lady took off her hat and scarf and slipped out of her coat. She folded her scarf about eight times, until it was the right size to shove into her hat. Then she crammed her stuffed hat into one of her coat-sleeves, rolled up the whole mess like a jellyroll, and stashed it away somewhere under the counter.

Using the little screen on the cash register as a mirror, she fluffed up her hair with her long red fingernails. Then she ducked out from behind the counter. I followed her around as she flipped on the light switches. I don't know why I followed her around, but I did. I do stuff like that all the time, then I say to myself, *what the heck did I do that for?* Anyway, all the while, in my heart I was screaming, *HURRY UP ALREADY!* Pretty soon, the lady ducked in to get behind the counter again. She reached into her purse for a little flip-open mirror and a tube of lipstick. Then she stretched her mouth into a big letter O and slowly painted her top lip—raspberry red. She smooshed her lips together to share the colour with her bottom lip then spread more raspberry on the bottom middle, where she'd missed the first time around. At last, she pressed her lips into a silent M over a Kleenex and threw her crushed-up kiss-mark into the garbage. *Why put it on if you're just gonna wipe it off?* The pendulum kept on going. Click—Click—Click—Click. The lady began to fiddle with the cash register. "You 'ave no school, ma'mselle?" said the raspberry mouth.

"Yes, I do. But it starts very late today." Then, I don't know why I went on and on, but I did. "My teacher had an appointment at the beauty parlour. Probably a cut and set. Maybe even one of those smelly perms."

The saleslady leaned on the counter. *"Vraiment?"*

"Well, she tried to make an appointment for three thirty, but they were all full-up. Boy, was she mad!"

"Incroyable! She tell you dat?"

"Well, she had to tell someone, and I just happened to be there." *Why did I even start?* I dropped my schoolbag to the floor. "I'm interested in buying a diary," I said.

"Which one? you know?"

"One with a little golden key."

"Dey all 'ave a gold key," she said.

"On a red ribbon?"

"Oui."

"And gold all around the edges?"

"Oui."

"I'd like one with a pretty design on the front...exactly like the one in the window...sitting on the fake snow under the tree."

She rummaged around in one of the great big drawers under the greeting card display then held up one of the diaries. "Dis one, ma'mselle?"

"Yes. Exactly."

She turned the key in the diary's lock a few times to make sure it was working and then re-wrapped it in the crinkled yellow tissue. I reached into the side pocket of my schoolbag and pulled out Deena's five dollar bill. The cash register clunked and dinged.

Then the lady snapped out the receipt. "*Trois quatre-vingt-dix-huit,*" she said.

The lady gave me my change and tucked the receipt into the small Waverly Gifts bag with my precious new diary. "Thank you," I said. "*Merci beaucoup.*"

"*Bienvenue,*" she answered. Then she shook her head and made some clicking sounds with her tongue.

I peeked at the cuckoo clock. *Here it is, fourteen minutes after nine. This is not the way I planned it!*

I tucked the diary into my schoolbag, headed for the door and waved. "*Bonjour, madame.*"

The wind chimes mocked me with their faint whispery chuckles as I stepped out into the frosty air.

The kids of Miss Barclay's third grade class were climbing ropes and swinging on the rings in the gym. I saw them as I glanced through the window to check the time. Nine twenty-six. Now what? *There's no way I'll walk into class at nine twenty-six.*

I headed away from school and around the corner. Hasky's was my only hope.

PLAN A: HASKY'S

Hasky's is mostly a cigar store, but it's also a snack bar, a candy store, a newspaper stand, and the best hangout in the neighbourhood. On Sundays you'd always find a few old guys sitting behind the counter, playing poker for nickels, and a whole bunch more playing chess way in the back room.

I balanced my schoolbag on one of the red stools at the soda counter and hoisted myself onto the seat beside it. The big brown ceiling fan click-clacked in a slow steady rhythm, chopping through the blue swirling smoke. A few men were sitting at a small round table, blowing smoke rings, drinking coffee and blaming Mayor Drapeau for all the snow removal problems. To their left, Mr. Haskell was playing the pinball machine. B-r-r-r-r...click...ding...ding...click. The noise suddenly stopped and the letters "T I L T" partly covered the partly uncovered lady on the motorcycle. Mr. Haskell flipped the flippers a half a dozen times, as if it would do him any good, then stepped behind the counter. "What can I do for you, young miss?"

I fished a quarter out of the side pocket of my schoolbag. "Just a cream soda, please."

He brought me a cream soda. "Anything else?"

"No, thank you. Do you mind if I sit here for a few minutes?"

Mr. Haskell slapped my change onto the rubber mat on the counter. "It's okay with me. Why should I mind?"

I hunted around for my ballpoint and notebook, tore out a page and wrote in my best handwriting:

Dear Mr. Peale,
Please excuse my daughter Vivian for being late for school this morgning

I scrunched up the note, stuffed it into my schoolbag and ripped out another page. With only a few pages left in the notebook, I knew that I had to concentrate on my spelling and handwriting this time around. Couldn't take any more chances!

Dear Mr. Peale,
Please excuse my daughter Vivian for being late for school this morning, as she had an erjent dentist appointment.
Yours truly,
Mrs. J. Glayzier

Mr. Haskell's white apron stopped in front of me. "U-R-G-E-N-T, not E-R-J-E-N-T," he said.

My heart sank into my stomach. I reached for another page.

"It's not gonna work, kid," he said. "I tried that once when I was your age, and it just doesn't work. Your handwriting is *your* handwriting. Your mother's handwriting is your *mother's* handwriting. Get it?"

"Yes," I said.

"What is it then? Y' late for school?"

"Y-yes." I felt my lower lip tug down, like I was going to start bawling any second.

"Aww, jeez. Why don't you just go? So...you'll be late. What's the worst thing that can happen, eh?"

"The Eleph...uhh...the principal, told me I'd be in big trouble if I came late one more time, because it would be my third 'late' in one month." Then, I took a chance. "Maybe you can help me...like...can you write me a note? You know...in a grown-up's handwriting?"

"Look, kid. I know you're heading for big trouble and all, but I can't bail you out." He swished a damp cloth over the counter and leaned toward me. "I'd really like to help you with this, but it's morally wrong. You know what that means?"

I nodded.

"Well, get along to school then," he said as he

whisked away my half-finished cream soda.

I picked up my schoolbag and left Hasky's. "My life is doomed," I cried. The heavy door clicked shut behind me. *I need a note. I need a note. What should I do?*

The telephone booth between the streetcar stop and the gas station smelled like a mixture of cold French fries, an ashtray and a toilet in the woods. In the shredded old phone book, I looked up Tzonvaytik, Joseph, on Park Avenue. I stuck a dime into the slot and dialed.

PLAN B:
DOCTOR TZONVAYTIK

I hate brown. Dr. Tzonvaytik's waiting room is positively brown. The walls are nylon stocking beige, the chairs are cocoa brown, and the carpet's like dark chocolate with little orange sprinkles.

Karen slid the glass window to one side. "I'm glad we could squeeze you in this morning. Please have a seat, Vivian."

I headed for my favourite chair, the one near the fish tank, and the first thing I did was reach into my schoolbag for my white leather diary. I unwrapped it. The fact that it wasn't real leather didn't matter at all because the cover had that fresh plastic smell, a bit like a new shower curtain. I took a couple of good whiffs. Then I closed my eyes and let my finger bump along the design around the border. I turned the pages, one at a time, carefully separating the ones that were stuck together by that gold stuff around the edges. At last, I turned all the way back to the inside of the front cover and wrote:

This diary belongs to Vivian Glayzier. I pity you if you steal this diary, for you will be judged harshly and will have to suffer the worst punishment. You may choose from the following:

❑ Mild pain
❑ Moderate pain
❑ Death

I re-wrapped the diary and put it back into my schoolbag. I rolled up my jacket and jammed it in over the diary.

Anybody who ever gets a good whiff of dental office would agree that it's not the same as hospital smell. It's worse. It goes right up your nostrils and makes everything close up as if you were saying "g" and "n" at the same time. Suddenly, I heard the screech of the drill, which actually made me wish I'd gone to school in the first place.

A pleasant voice called, "Vivian?" It was Audrey, the skinny nurse who always drowns herself in about half-a-gallon of Evening in Paris.

"C'mon into room three. I'll get you ready," said Audrey.

I followed her into room three. I hate room three about as much as I hate room one and room two. Audrey motioned for me to sit in the brown leather chair. She pumped the chair up...up...up, until I was high enough off the ground to consider it dangerous. Then she adjusted the headrest. I don't get it. Those headrest things are always too high or too low, so sometimes they squash my skull and sometimes they fold my ears in half. That day, the headrest made me feel as if my head was lopsided. Audrey clipped a paper bib into place and swung the tray of dentist tools toward me. I checked them over to see if they were slimy or clean. I always do that because I never know if anybody really bothers to clean them up them between patients.

"Got a toothache?" said Audrey.

I straightened my bib. "Yes. A bad one."

"When did it start?"

"A...a few months ago."

"A few months? Why didn't you call for an appointment way back then?"

"W-well. It went away. Just came back this morning."

When Audrey left the room, I checked out the stuff on the tray again and then counted the drawers of the cabinet under the window. *Three times six is eighteen. Eighteen tiny drawers for drills, cotton puffs, and probably a little crunching machine to grind up the silvery stuff for fillings—the stuff that always ends up at the back of your throat, and you can't figure out if it's better to spit it out or swallow it.*

While I waited, I watched the water swish around in the little whirlpool sink beside me. I reached for the Dixie cup full of Lavoris and rinsed my mouth. Then I cleared my throat...and spat. Khaaap-ptoo! My spit wouldn't shake loose and just dangled off my bottom lip like a hunk of rope. So I transferred it to the end of my finger and swung it back and forth over the sink, hoping to set it free. That's when Dr. Tzonvaytik walked in and startled me. My spit hit the floor, and I died of embarrassment. What if he'd seen it? If not, maybe he'd heard the "splat". He didn't say anything, but that didn't stop me from worrying that he might slip on it and go flying.

Dr. Tzonvaytik adjusted the big bright light until it was shining in my eyes, then he picked up his little mirror-on-a-stick. "So, what brings you here today?"

"A terrible toothache."

He carefully picked out just the right poking stick from the tray. "Let's see how terrible. Open wide." He tapped on one of my big teeth way at the back. "Does that hurt?"

"Unh-unh."

He tapped the next one. "How about that?"

"Unh-unh."

He continued tapping. "That?"

"Unh-unh."

He went on tapping every bottom tooth. Then he

started on the top ones. "Does that hurt?"

"Unh-unh."

"That?"

"Unh-unh."

Then I figured he'd soon run out of teeth, so the next time he tapped, I screamed, "AHH-H-H-H-H!"

He started poking around on my gums with a much pointier torture-stick. The hair in his nose trembled every time he breathed in and out.

"Well. You say you have a toothache, Vivian, but there doesn't appear to be any swelling or even the slightest sign of a problem."

"Maybe the swelling's way underneath the tooth," I said.

He shook his head. "No chance of that."

"Maybe the tooth looks okay, but it's actually gone all rotten on the inside."

"Very unlikely," he said.

"I chewed tons of Fleer's Double Bubble last week. Maybe some got inside. Just squeezed in under the gums. I think I read somewhere that gum can do that."

He frowned. "I guess I didn't receive *that* issue of the *Journal of Dentistry.*"

"I hate to admit it, but I hardly brushed anywhere near that tooth since my last visit."

He curled the corners of his mouth down and

squinted. "So, what do you think I should do, Vivian? Think I should freeze your gums with a big needle and pull the tooth out with a huge pair of pliers?"

"Well...no."

"Okay, then. How about if I just apply some of this nice-smelling red stuff? Aha! That's what I'll do." He rubbed the red stuff on my teeth and gums with a little swab. The smell was terrible and the taste was even worse. Then he stuck a roll of cotton, about the size of my thumb, between my tooth and cheek. "Well, Vivian. How's that feel?"

"Vuch vetter. Vuch, vuch vetter. Hank you."

Audrey lowered the chair and set me free. I threw on my jacket, grabbed my schoolbag and flew out onto Park Avenue. I ran all the way back to school, wheezing like a fire truck. Just outside my classroom, I reached up to feel the bulge in my cheek. *The note! The note! I forgot to ask for a note!*

BACKFIRE!

I turned the knob very slowly and carefully pulled the door open—just wide enough to sneak into the classroom. Mr. Byers was cutting a blackboard pie into six equal parts. The clock over the world map said eleven fifteen.

I tiptoed to my desk. All eyes were on me. Mr. Byers' chalk squawked to a halt in the middle of a fraction. He looked over his shoulder and stared. "Whom do we have here?" he said.

"I Wiwian," I said pointing to the bulge in my cheek. "Can't talk."

"Why are you late for class?"

I pointed into my mouth.

"Did you bring a note from your dentist?"

"Ah 'orgot."

He began to brush chalk dust from the front of his navy jacket, leaving more chalk-dust than there was before. "You forgot? You forgot to get a note? In that case you must report to Mr. Peale's office at once." He turned to face the class. "Now, where were we?" He snapped a fresh piece of chalk in half and began to screech a new fraction onto the blackboard.

Mr. Peale was wearing his dark grey suit. Its wrinkles had wrinkles of their own. He motioned me to a chair. "Sit down, Vivian." He tilted himself way back. Then he wove his fingers together like a little basket and just sat there. I waited. Nothing. I reached down and nervously began to twist the top of my sock around my finger. The Elephant took his glasses from his pocket and unfolded them. Holding onto one of the earpieces, he let the glasses dangle loosely between his fingers. No words. Just his glasses sweeping back and forth like a pendulum and him staring across the desk like an owl. I gave my sock an extra few twists. *Is he waiting for me to speak first?* He suddenly sprang forward in his chair. His voice thundered: "WELL?"

I jumped up...and fell onto Mr. Peale's desk. Splat! His family photos skated to the edge of the desk—and plunged to the floor. Pens and pencils flew in every direction. When I straightened up, I saw a most surprised look on Mr. Peale's face, and his desk blotter squashing a dent into his stomach. I slithered to the floor and untangled my finger from the big fat knot I had twisted into my sock.

Mr. Peale and I got down on all fours to sweep up his pens and pencils. I couldn't help but notice how much like an elephant he really looked at that moment. Out of the blue, a laugh gathered up somewhere inside me and then burst. "H-A-A-A-A!" The roll of cotton popped out of my mouth and tumbled out of reach.

"You're taking this all too lightly, Miss Glayzier."

I passed him a ruler and two rubber bands. "Oh, no, Mr. Peale," I said. "I always laugh when I'm upset. My doctor's quite concerned."

His hairy fingers raked a bunch of paper clips into a little pile. "Perhaps I should have a word with your doctor," he said, chasing a pencil stub around the leg of his desk. "What's his name?"

I cringed. "Who?"

"Your doctor, Vivian. Your doctor."

"Oh, yes. My doctor. Uhh...Dr. Kent. Dr. Clark...Kent."

The Elephant seemed to perk up. "Clark Kent, Vivian? As in Superman?"

"Oh. Right. How foolish of me to get all mixed up like that. It's Kent Clarke, with an 'e' at the end."

"And, can you tell me, Miss Glayzier...where this Dr. Kent Clarke's office is?"

"Uh...in a clinic. Yes, that's it. It's right near a post office, or a fire station, I think. He moved, though. Sometime last week. Just scooped up his stethoscope and examining table, a bunch of needles and maybe some of those wooden sticks for saying 'a-a-a-h'. Then he skipped town. They say he had to, 'cause he fell way behind in his rent."

Mr. Peale turned his head sideways with a slight smile. "One day I'd sure like to get the lowdown on Dr. Clarke's sudden disappearance. Go on now! Get a pass from Miss Cooper and hurry back to your classroom before the day is over."

MOM CONFRONTS VIVIAN

~~Friday, January 1, 1954~~
Thursday, December 16th, 1954

Dear Diary,

I got swindled! Royally cheated! Instead of selling me a brand new diary, the Waverly lady sold me one of last year's leftovers—and 1954's almost over! And to make matters worse, I've already written in it—in ink...so even if I tried, I'd never get my money back! The fact is...I'll be filling in my own dates anyway, so I won't bother losing any sleep over it.

I'm Vivian Glayzier. I'll soon be twelve. On April Fools' Day to be exact, and that's not even funny. I'm the only person in the whole school stuck with a creepy name like Vivian and that's not funny either. In my whole life I never even met another Vivian. If Mom and Dad were really so hung up on a "V" name, they could have picked something with more kick in it, like Valencia, or Valentina. We've got a whole bunch of Carols and Nancys in my school. I know at least a half-a-dozen Deenas, (four Deenas with two e's, one Dena with only one e, and one Dina spelled with an i.) We have three Cathys with a "C" and two Kathys with a "K". And the most popular name in the whole school is definitely Barbara...and they all wish they could skate like Barbara Ann Scott...HA!

I have no brothers and no sisters, which makes me an only child—100% no fair! My mother is Jenny and my father is Dan but that doesn't really matter any more because soon they'll be divorced—if I don't figure out a way to stop them!

I hate school. It's especially because of the teachers, and the one I hate most is Shipwreck-Shevarek. Today was an exception because she saved my life. I got into a heap of trouble with her yesterday because I wrote a note (about her!) in class. Then she sent me to The Elephant (Mr. Peale).

Last night I did something so despicable. Most people would probably get locked up for it. Anyway, I must go now...Mom just came home and she's calling me in "that" voice!

— Valentina V. Glayzier

I helped Mom lug three grocery bags from the front door into the kitchen. "What on earth is going on, Vivian?"

"I don't know what's going on," I said. "So you may as well tell me. And if you think I'm too young or too stupid to know, it's a big mistake. I'm old enough to know everything...absolutely everything!"

"Me tell *you?* No, Miss Sassafras. I want you to tell me. What the heck were you doing at the dentist this morning? Can you answer that?"

"I had a bad toothache." *How did she find out?*

"A toothache?" She yanked the fridge door open hard enough to make all the jars and bottles clunk and rattle. "How come I wasn't aware of your toothache?"

"Well, toothaches happen when you least expect them, Mom, and this toothache just up and happened."

Mom crammed the celery and carrots into the vegetable bin. "I don't buy that story, Vivian."

"Well, I had one anyway. How did you find out that I went to the dentist?"

"I'm the one asking the questions here, young lady. And what do you mean, 'you had one anyway'?"

I knew Mom would never let up. I took a deep breath. "Well, I guess I...faked a toothache."

Mom spun around. She stood straight up then leaned toward me with her face an inch from mine. I hate it when she does that. "You guess you *faked* a toothache? Can you take out a minute from your fidgeting to explain that one to me? Can you take out one minute to tell me why Audrey had to call from the dental office to ask how you're doing?"

"Promise you won't yell?"

"Go ahead. I won't yell," said Mom in her almost-yelling voice.

"Promise?"

"Vivian. I'm *not* in the mood for your games," she said.

I took a deep breath. *Here goes.* "I was afraid to walk into class late again. I decided to fake a toothache so I could go to the dentist in a big hurry. That way I'd be able to get a note to bring to class—and still stay out of trouble."

"You mean you went to *all that trouble* to stay out of trouble? Was it worth it? Well, was it?"

"No, it wasn't worth it. I forgot to ask for a note and ended up in Mr. Peale's office after all."

Mom continued to empty the grocery bags and chased after an apple that escaped her grip. It rolled into the dining room. We both followed. "You left for school much earlier than usual, Vivian. For heaven's sake, how could you have been late?"

"Uh...I went over to Waverly Gifts and...well...time just flew. You know how time flies."

"Waverly Gifts? Before school? They don't even open until nine!"

"I know. I mean, I didn't know it then, but I know it now. Once I got there, I decided to wait until they opened. My angel sure didn't try hard enough to stop me."

"Don't go blaming your angel. Can you tell me why it was so important to go to Waverly Gifts?"

"I went to check out the window display," I said.

"O-h-h-h? If you were just checking out the window display, why did you have to wait until they opened?"

"Uh-h..."

"Uh-h? Is that all you can say?" Her voice was starting to get louder again.

"Well, one thing led to another," I said, "and I was propelled to go inside."

"Compelled, Vivian. You know that was very irresponsible of you!"

"I'm sorry, Mom."

"I hope you are! And I guarantee you that you'll be a lot sorrier when the bill comes in for your fake toothache."

THE "OTHER WOMAN"

~~Saturday, January 2, 1954~~
Friday, December 17th, 1954

Dear Diary,

Not much time to write. I have to get ready to leave for school in three minutes so I won't have to deal with The Elephant again. While I was having breakfast, I found out about the divorce! Not from Mom. Not from Dad. No. The evidence was right on the kitchen table—in yesterday's newspaper! I couldn't believe what I saw. It made me sick! Now I know! It's all his fault, and I'll never forgive him as long as I live. So on top of all my other troubles, now I have to figure out what to do about Bernice.

– Valencia G

*　　*　　*

Deena stopped at my locker. "Got your book report done?"

"Nope. We still have tons of time."

"We have to hand them in today, you know."

"Nice try, Deena. It's due *next* week."

"I'm not kidding, Viv. The deadline's *today!* Is your brain having a nice vacation?"

"Dang! I hardly even started reading the book. Deena...quick! Tell me what it's about. Just a short synopsis. I'll do the report at recess."

"You nuts? You can't do a report if you didn't even read the book, you moron."

Everybody was so flipped out about this Tolkien guy. Well, the fact is, I had too much on my mind to worry about The Rabbit or The Habbit or whatever. Anyway, I had more important things to do than waste a perfectly good recess on writing a book report.

Mr. Byers' class seemed to drag on endlessly, and the math problems were driving me bats! I read them over and over, getting more confused each time.

At nine o'clock, train "A" starts its journey from Montreal to Toronto, traveling at 80 miles per hour. At the same time, train "B" sets out from Toronto to Montreal, traveling at 76 miles per hour. The distance between the two cities is 390 miles. At what time will the two trains meet?

I scribbled a whole pageful of equations but couldn't come up with the answer. Actually, I wasn't too sure that I even understood the question. But on the odd chance that this was another one of Mr. Byers' trick questions, I wrote: "The trains will never meet because they're on different tracks." While I waited for the class to end, I made up my own math problem, one that I've been thinking about ever since our school trip to Ottawa last year.

A passenger train is zipping along the track at one hundred miles per hour. There's a fly in the train, buzzing around at three miles per hour. Why is it that the fly doesn't get itself smashed up against the back window of the train?

Every now and then I reached into my pocket to make sure the little scrap of newspaper was still in there. I had my next move all planned, but I just needed the hands on the clock to spin around a whole lot faster.

I could tell from the way the other kids' pencils were scratching along the pages that they all knew what they were doing. I just sat there like a piece of meat with eyes. What really gets me is that most teachers don't know how to make the work interesting enough, so it's really *their* fault if you can't concentrate. For instance, they'll finish off a sentence, but then as soon as they start into the next one, you're danged if you remember what they told you a split second earlier. And when they write things on the blackboard, it's hard to follow along because your brain's all clogged up with other stuff, like how cool they write their bs and ds, or how they cross their ts without slanting up or down all over the place. And what about Mr. Byers? He always starts off too far to the right, so before you know it, he's got us wondering if he'll end up squeezing all his equations into the edge of the blackboard again.

At last! The recess bell. I couldn't get to the door fast enough. The halls were jammed with kids shuffling off in all directions. I made a beeline for the main door and ran to the stinky phone booth around the corner.

There was a fifth-grader yakking away in there while digging down into his Cracker Jacks for the prize. Just outside the booth, a lady was poking around in her purse, fishing for small change.

After what seemed like forever, the kid finally hung up and raced down the street. The lady planted herself inside the phone booth and creaked the door shut.

I paced up and down the sidewalk, as if, by some magic, that would free up the phone for me. *Say goodbye, Mrs. Chatterbox. Hang up right now! Okay, you get one more chance. I'm gonna head over to that stop sign over there, and by the time I get back, you'd better be outta there.*

I took about a hundred chicken-steps toward the stop sign then spun around. She was gone! But by then, somebody else had taken her place and was busy dialing.

My turn came...at long last! The phone booth had that surefire smell of Cracker Jacks. The receiver was coated with fluff, red woolly fluff pulled free from Mrs. Chatterbox's gloves, trapped in sticky caramel. I plunked in my coin, held up the snippet of newspaper, and carefully dialed the number. Pick up the phone, Bernice. You're in for it now, you big dumb floozy!

THE ELEPHANT
LENDS AN EAR

"Good morning. Miss Villner's office."

"Good morning. Is there somebody there called Bernice?"

"Yes. Bernice Villner."

"May I speak with her please?"

"Certainly. Who's calling please?"

"Tell her it's...uh-h...Mrs. Glayzier."

"One moment please."

I heard typewriters clacking away in the background while I waited and waited. *How long does it take Bernice Villner to get to the phone? I don't have all day. Bare-Knees Villner. Bare-Knees-the-Villain. That's more like it.*

"Good morning. Miss Villner speaking."

"I'll get right to the point, Miss Villner." My voice began to shake. "You just stay away from Dan Glayzier. Do you hear me?"

"Oh my! What's this all about?"

"None of your beeswax. I just want you to know that he was very happy till now. He doesn't need you,

67

so just leave well enough alone!"

"W-why, this is most unusual."

"So be it, Miss Villner. Just keep your clammy claws off of him. Get the point?"

I didn't wait for an answer. I just slammed the phone down. *I hope that rattled your feeble discombobulated cootie-brain!*

The Elephant was having a little smokeroo beside the main door, half-hidden by one of the pillars. By the time I noticed him, it was too late to turn back. When he saw me, he checked his watch and then threw his head back. "Not again!"

"I was here this morning, I really was," I said. "I tried to make it back on time, but...the eulogy seemed to go on forever."

"The eulogy?"

"Yes. My poor grandmother. She caught some kind of flu or something. Just hit her like a ton of bricks and she...didn't quite make it."

"Vivian. Tell me if I'm wrong, but I think you've gone through about a half a dozen grandmothers over the last few years. You'll have to think up something much more convincing than that. In any case, let's not waste precious time on formalities today. I'll walk you back to your classroom."

He crushed the lit end of his cigar against the bricks and stamped out the little sparks that had fallen to the cement. "Now, can you tell me what *really* happened, Vivian?"

"I needed to make an important phone call. That's what really happened, Mr. Peale." *It feels so good to get the truth out. I hate it when I have to make up stories. Stories? Who am I kidding? They're not stories—they're lies. Lies. Lies. Not just fibs or "stretching-the-truth" as Mom would say. They're big fat lies.*

"If it was such an important phone call, you know Miss Cooper would have let you use the office telephone. Why didn't you just come into the office?"

"It had to be private, Mr. Peale. I couldn't take the chance of having anyone listen in."

He stopped walking and bent to face me. "Has something been troubling you lately?"

"No," I said. Then my throat started to close up.

"I do believe something's upsetting you, Vivian. Let's stop off at your classroom. I'll explain to the teacher that you'll join the class later on. But right now I think it's best that we go into my office and have a little chat."

The sun flowed through the venetian blinds and covered Mr. Peale with black and white stripes. *What do you get when you cross an elephant with a zebra?* He motioned for me to sit down and flopped himself into his big swivel chair. He brought his hands down heavily on his desk, sending dust particles to dance in the sunlight. His eyes looked serious but friendly. "Please. Tell me what's troubling you, Vivian. Maybe I can help."

I ran my fingers along the deep grain of the old wooden desk. "I don't know how to tell you," I said.

His voice sounded soft. "Just start from the beginning, Vivian."

"I...I don't even know where the beginning is."

"Then tell me whatever you can. The middle is okay for a start."

"It's...it's my father."

He looked concerned. "Your father? Is he all right?"

"I can't explain it," I said. I felt like making a dash for it.

"Do you think you can try?"

I looked down into my lap. It seemed to take forever until the words came out. "He's carrying on, you know."

"Carrying on? I'm not sure I understand what you mean, Vivian."

"Divorce. My parents are getting a divorce."

"Oh, Vivian. I'm so sorry to hear this," he said. "You must have found it quite upsetting when they told you about it."

"I'm upset, all right. But we didn't get to discuss it yet. They hardly ever talk about stuff like that. They never even say words like 'dead' or...or...'pregnant' so for sure they'd never say...you know...'divorce'. But it's no secret. They'd had a big fight while I was over at my Grandpa's. When I got home, sure as I'm sitting here, my Dad sprang it on Mom that he was leaving. Then this morning, just before I dug into my Corn Flakes, I started flipping through yesterday's Star, looking for 'Little Orphan Annie'. That's when I found out about the 'other woman'."

"The other woman?"

I unfolded the little scrap of newspaper and smoothed it out in front of Mr. Peale. I showed him where Dad had scribbled Bernice's name and number. "See? Look at this," I said, pointing to the tiny words he'd written in the margin beside her name: "Very attractive! Awfully tempting!"

A FRANTIC CALL
FROM GRANDPA

Mom pulled the oven door open. A ribbon of steam brought a little bit of Italy right into our kitchen. Homemade pizza. A new recipe Mom had snipped out of one of the magazines at her doctor's office.

Olive oil trickled between the craters of melted cheese. No one spoke much.

Dad picked away at his crust.

Just look at him. His mind's probably on Bare-Knees-the-Villain. Pretty soon I'm gonna let him know what I think about the whole thing. I don't care any more.

I was bursting to talk about what was going on with *them*. And I wanted to tell *them* what was going on with *me*, but I couldn't think of how to begin. Then the phone rang. "Blast!" said Dad as he reached to answer it.

"Hello...say, Pop. How's it goin'?...What?...You sure?... Come on, now. Your place is such a mess, you couldn't find a giraffe with a raspy throat... When did you use it last? Maybe you wanna check around again and call me back... Sure thing... Speak to you later, Pop."

I started to line up a few strips of green pepper on the rim of my plate. By the time Dad hung up, the guilt was bouncing around inside me like a ping-pong ball.

Dad shook his head. "His place is such a bloody mess," he muttered. "No wonder he can never find anything."

Mom rolled her eyes. "What's he lost now?" she said wearily.

Dad shrugged. "His pen. Probably misplaced it."

Mom frowned. "Your Pop's got pens all over the place. Why's he so frantic about a pen?"

"It's not just any old pen," said Dad. "It's the one Mama gave him four years ago—on their anniversary. It was her final gift to him before she passed away."

ONCE UPON A MOUNTAIN

~~Sunday, January 3, 1954~~
Saturday, December 18, 1954

Oh dear! Oh dear! Oh! Dear Diary,

I'm in the middle of the worst week of my entire life. Everything's gone wrong. Last night Dad got a telephone call from Grandpa, who's now busy turning his whole house upside down and inside out, looking for his pen.

Also, they think they're doing me a big favour by keeping me in the dark. It's not like I'm a two-year-old or anything. The least they could do is tell me what's going on so I could plan my life...which is all tangled up anyway. Well, I'm glad I called Bare-Knees-the-Villain. Maybe now Dad will come to his senses.

Another problem is that there's a ton of snow out there and that means we're going to the mountain today. I shouldn't complain. At least it'll give me a chance to get the pen back from Deena.

– Valencia V. Glayzier

＊　　＊　　＊

We got to the mountain early, just as planned, before it got crammed with kids. "The perfect day!" I said, brushing a heavy coating of freshly fallen snow from one of the lion statues.

The last time we'd gone to the mountain was in late November. It was after a doozy of a snowfall, and it was so cold, we could see our breath. I swear, it must have been about twenty below. Just around the time we thought we'd freeze to death out there, Shelly had announced. "Let's go for a hot chocolate—my treat."

Mr. Davidson had topped our hot chocolates with great gobs of whipped cream and even slipped a few tea biscuits onto our saucers. It was like cloud nine!

Then Shelly had unzipped the pocket of her fur-trimmed ski-jacket to pull out a ten-dollar bill. While she was counting her change, she said, "We've gotta do this again real soon."

"Great idea!" said Deena. "And next time it's *your* treat. Okay, Viv?"

Well—my treat-day had finally arrived. We left the lion statues and raced to our favourite hill. The sun was shining its brightest, so that if you stared at the snow on the ground long enough, you could see the most amazing sparkle of green and pink. We dragged our sleds up the hills and glided down, over and over, shrieking and laughing until our voices began to crumble. Clumps of ice stuck to my mitts, and snowflakes whooshed their way into my boots and up into my sleeves.

After a while, we pulled our sleds across the road to the old playground on Fletcher's Field, our boots crunching and squeaking in the snow. We cleared off the swings, sat down and began kicking our boots against the snow, first to the left, then to the right, over and over until we were all swinging in choppy figures-of-eight. Between the steady squawk of the rusty chains, I could still hear the noisy kids on the hills across the way. Shelly stopped her swing and flopped herself backward into the snow a few feet away. "Look! A snow angel!" she shouted.

I took a deep breath and called over to Deena, "I need the gold pen back."

"You what?"

"You heard me right," I said. "I need the pen back."

She laughed. "You must be joking! I already gave it to my grandfather, you creep, and I'd rather croak than ask him for it."

My heart sank. "Well, it's too bad, Deena. You've

gotta get it from him. I mean it."

"Forget it! Do you know how stupid it is to give somebody a present and then ask for it back?"

My throat went dry. "Please, Deena. Please ask him for it. I need that pen. I need it now!"

She didn't answer.

Lying face-up in her perfectly formed snow angel, Shelly called up to the treetops, "Who's ready for hot chocolate?"

"Me! Me!" said Deena.

I leaned my sled against a tree and reached into the back pocket of my snow pants. Then I checked the other back pocket. Then the front pockets. In a minute my hands flew into each of my jacket pockets and I screamed, "It's gone! My money's gone!"

"Gone?" said Shelly. "What do you mean, gone?"

"Gone means gone," I said. "I must have dropped it. We've just got to find it!"

Deena frowned. "You crazy? It's like looking for a needle in..."

"It's probably in the snow," I said. "Maybe over at the lions."

"The lions! You gone nuts?" said Deena. "You want us to walk all the way back to the lions?"

When we got to the lions, Deena said, "Now that you made us walk all the way back here, we're gonna comb every square inch of this mountain, even if it takes us till midnight!"

"How much did you have?" said Shelly.

"Three dollars," I said. "Maybe it blew away or something."

"Well, we'll just have to keep on looking," said Shelly.

"Maybe somebody found it," I said. "Some lucky stiff probably went ahead and found my three bucks."

We looked all around the area near the lions. Then we walked back to Mount Royal, climbing all the little hills to look for three dollars in the snow. "Cripe! I'll die if we don't find it," I said. But by then the wind had picked up, and I was too cold and too wet to go on any further. I sat down on my sled.

"C'mon, Viv," said Shelly. "We'll help you find it. We will. We'll continue looking until we find it. I promise."

"FOR-GET IT!" said Deena. "She probably *never* even had any money to begin with. She just made us freeze out here for nothing!" Then Deena turned to whisper something to Shelly, and they just left the scene. I stood up to join them.

"You're on your own, you brainless nitwit," said Deena. "We never want to talk to *you* again. You're nothing but a big nothing...zero-minus...a sorry excuse for a friend."

They ran ahead of me, their sleds bumping along

behind them. Every once in a while, they swung around and snickered. Each burst of laughter slashed into me deeper and deeper—like a sword. I felt my throat tighten up until my cries got squeezed into a painful knot.

Vivian Confronts Mom

Rosemary Clooney was belting out "This Ole House" on the Hit Parade while Mom's crochet hook kept pouring out afghan. In the quiet of my own room, I flipped on the gooseneck lamp and turned to page twenty-eight of *The Hobbit*. I had way over half-an-inch of reading left to get me to the back cover, or to be exact, another two hundred and eighty-four pages. I could have picked out another Hardy Boys or Cherry Ames or something, but NO! Stupid copycat me—I had to take out the same book as Deena!

The phone rang. "Will somebody get that," shouted Mom from the living room."

I was the only other "somebody" in the house besides Mom, so I ran into the kitchen and grabbed the phone. "Hello."

"Vivi?"

The sound of Shelly's voice made my heart jump. "I thought you were never talking to me again."

"Look, Viv. That wasn't my idea. It was Deena's. I

know I was a jerk for walking out on you at the mountain. And anyway, that was *her* idea too. But I've had it with her. You know what she said? She said, 'If you ever speak to that Vivian Glayzier again, I'll drop you as a friend forever'."

"So, how come you called?"

"Because I felt like it, Viv—and she could just keep her nose out of my business."

"You mean you don't care if she drops you as a friend forever?"

"Don't you get it, Viv? She's bad news. She's not a real friend anyway—she never was."

"I thought you two were best friends, Shelly."

"In her mind! She thinks that just because she's so popular she can run the world. Well, I have news for *her*. She can't run *me* any more."

"Me neither," I said.

"Anyway, Viv, I think she was the most rotten of rottens today...the way she spoke to you."

"Do you think she was right, though? You know, about me making you guys search the whole mountain for nothing?"

"Actually, I thought it was awful that you lost your money, and I felt really bad for you."

Mom burst into the kitchen. "You still busy yakking? I thought you would have started on your homework by now."

"Sorry. I can't talk right now. I gotta go."

Mom started clearing some dishes from the drain board. "Who was that?" she asked.

"It was Shelly...my very last friend in the whole world. The whole solar system!"

"Oh, don't start getting dramatic, Vivian."

"Well, it's true. Everybody hates me. I'm a big fat zero. Zilch...to the tenth power."

The phone rang again. I glanced at Mom.

"Well, go ahead and answer it," she said, a touch of impatience creeping into her voice.

"Hello."

"Sorry, Viv. It's me again. I want you to know how crummy I feel about what happened today. Can you call me later? Or—better still—why don't you come over for a bit?"

"Hold on a sec," I said and squooshed the phone against myself to block out the conversation. "Mom?"

"What is it this time?"

"Mom, can I go over to Shelly's for a while?"

"Shelly's? All the way up in Outremont! You know your father's not home, Vivian. How do you suppose you'll get there? How will you get home?"

I twirled the phone wire. "Do you know when Dad's coming back?"

"Are you kidding? Saturday night? You expect him to be home on a Saturday night? He's probably planted himself outside the furniture store again to watch hockey on television. He'd rather freeze out there with all those other lunatics than listen to the game on the radio."

"Shelly?"

"Can you, Vivi? Can you come over?"

"No. I can't."

"Well then, if you want, I can come to *your* house. I know my Mom wouldn't mind, and I'm sure Gary would give me a lift. Boy! Since he got his license, he'll use any excuse to take the car."

"Mom, can Shelly visit for a bit if her brother can give her a ride?"

"Of course, Vivian. I'm okay with that."

Shelly's Mom gave her the green light. I was thrilled—for about five seconds! Shelly had never come over to *my* place before. I ran around trying to picture the house through Shelly's eyes, and I didn't like what "she" saw. Shelly's house always smells of Johnson's wax and freshly baked raisin bread. Nothing's *ever* messy at Shelly's, and there's no dust anywhere. Ever. I needed to act fast. I gathered up all the boots and shoes at the entrance and tossed them into the back of the closet. I dragged the rubber mat out from under the chesterfield and unrolled it over the worn-out carpet at the front door. Next—the bathroom. I pulled the shower curtain closed, cleaned the sink with Old Dutch and gave the toilet a quick scrub with the curvy brush. Onward to the kitchen. I trapped all the floor crumbs with a wet Kleenex—especially those trying to hide in the corners—and sent them down the drain. Another quick look around the living room. No time to vacuum! I picked up all the little bits of fluff that didn't blend into the carpet, tossed them into the toilet and flushed them away.

From grungy to gorgeous in seven easy steps. Nothing like Shelly's place, but it'll have to do.

* * *

Shelly sprawled out on my bed with one leg draped over the footboard. If she saw the collection of dead flies up there in the light fixture, she was just too polite to say anything about it. I was hoping she hadn't seen the cobweb dangling in the corner over my desk.

Just then Shelly said, "What's that stringy thing up there?"

"No big deal," I said. "Just a cobweb."

Her eyes widened. "What the heck's a cob?"

I was sorry she asked. I didn't have a decent explanation, because even though I've always wondered about cobwebs myself, I've never bothered to ask anyone. "Must be another name for a spider," I said.

I'm a real Miss Muffet when it comes to spiders. But even though they scare the heck out of me, there's something about them—something scientific—that puzzles me the most. The maple tree's at least five feet away from the fence. We're not talking inches here. You're strolling along, and this web hits you right across your mouth. How can the spider get the thread going horizontal like that? This is what I think: the spider just drops a line from the tree branch. Straight down. Hangs there and waits for a wind to come along, a wind that's strong enough to get him swinging like Tarzan on a vine. Whoosh! He grabs onto the fence and voilà! A horizontal web—usually at mouth level.

"I sure hope your mom's taking things okay," said Shelly. "Like I hope she doesn't go all goofy or depressed or anything."

"Me too," I said. "It always starts off as a big nothing. Just a regular argument over one stupid thing or another, and pretty soon the whole thing gets totally out of hand. Most of the time they get over it, but not this time. The truth is, their marriage couldn't get any more crummy than it is right now. It's doomed."

I sat on the floor and began to pick out my favourite records to stack on the phonograph. "Anyway, you'd think by now they would have said something, wouldn't you? What really bugs me is how they go on pretending that things are so ho-hum-normal around here. Do they think I'm too stupid to know what's going on?"

"Oh, Viv. You have every right to know. If I were you, I'd sit them both down and tell them to give you the whole miserable lowdown. Maybe they're not even sure how to break the news to you. Maybe they're afraid you'd go bonkers or something."

"I know, I know. I guess part of me doesn't really want to hear what they have to say anyway. But you're right, Shelly. It's been three whole days now, and it's darn well time to get it out into the open. First thing tomorrow, whether they like it or not, they'll have me to answer to."

We played "Sh-boom" and "Mr. Sandman" over and over again. Then I began to sing along with Kay Starr. My hairbrush made a dandy microphone.

"Oh, we ain't got a barrel of...money,
Maybe we're ragged and...funny,
But we'll travel along,
Singin' a song,
Side by side.
Don't know what's comin' tomorrow
Maybe it's trouble and...sorrow..."

Shelly let her head hang off the edge of the bed and

looked at me upside down. "She's mad as a hornet, you know."

"Who, Deena?"

"Yes. Her Royal High-Falootin' Highness, Princess Margarine herself."

"She say why?"

"Yeah. She said she was sure you were lying today. You know...about losing your money and all that. She said you're from the wrong side of the tracks—whatever that means—and that you don't even have two nickels to rub together."

I slipped "Sh-boom" back into its sleeve. "You believe her?"

She turned to face the window. "Naw. Not really. W-well...maybe just a bit."

I felt like curling up into a ball and rolling under the bed. *Oh, no! Don't let Shelly turn on me too. She's the only friend I have left!*

Shelly sat up and crossed her legs like a pretzel. "Just forget it, Vivi. It doesn't even matter."

"What do you mean 'it doesn't matter'? Of course it matters. Go ahead and tell me. I won't get mad. Jeez. I swear on a hundred bibles, I won't get mad."

Shelly started to pick away at the skin around her fingernails. She probably wanted to take her words back, but it was too late. "Well, at first, I guess I didn't believe her," she said. "But then, I figured, well... I know your Dad drives an old jalopy and all that...you know, all rusty...no whitewalls...and you don't have a TV or anything, so I figured maybe she's right...s-sort of."

I couldn't answer. I looked around my room. What a garbage heap! My night table—just an old orange crate that we found in front of the grocery store. I'd spent practically a whole day sanding the wood until it was almost smooth. After giving it two coats of yellow paint, I'd felt like I was on top of the world. My dresser used to be Grandma Rosie's. It's old and brown and awfully scratched up, but when Dad brought it home for me, I felt I had everything I ever needed. I knew Shelly was comparing my room to hers. I knew that, in her eyes, my room was a total junkyard. My heart began to melt and sink lower and lower.

Shelly stared at the floor. "I'm sorry. I'm so sorry," she said. "I hope you're not mad at me now, Vivi. I guess I shouldn't have said anything—me and my big mouth!"

"Darn it, Shelly. Now I'll bet you think I'm just a poor old nothing."

"Never, Vivi! Never. Why would you even think that?"

"I suppose 'cause my place is such a dump."

"Aw, come off it, Vivi! You just don't get it. You're one of the lucky ones. You get to fix up your room just the way you like it. My parents would kill me if I tried that.

They'd ship me off to reform school. I wouldn't even dream of jazzing up my walls with clips of John Derek and Marlon Brando. Oh, man! They're so gorgeous!"

"You mean it? You really think my room's okay?"

"Okay's not the word for it, Vivi. It's dynamite!"

*   *   *

Saturday, December 18, 1954 (again)

Dear Diary,

Boy! Was I wrong! I can't believe I ever wanted to be best friends with Deena. She's like a thorn. Not like Shelly. Shelly has no sharp edges at all. She's more like hand lotion, cool and soft. Not many people I know are like hand lotion. Actually, most people I know are half-and-half. Thorns one day and hand lotion the next—and I never know what to expect from them.

– Valentina aka VVN

I hated to see Shelly go, but Gary came by for her just after nine thirty. I brushed my teeth, got into pyjamas and made a stopover at The Crochet Machine.

"O-oh, I see you're all set for bed," said Mom.

"Calling it an early night?"

I stretched out beside Mom's chair. "Maybe I'll read a bit first," I said, opening up *The Hobbit* for the umpteenth time. *I'll never finish this darn thing. I swear, seems like every time I turn my back, they keep on adding more and more pages!*

I stuck the bookmark back in at page twenty-eight. "Mom, do you still love him?"

"Who?"

"Dad."

"What kind of a question is that?"

"Well. Do you? Do you love him...even though?"

The thorns seemed to be creeping into her voice. "What do you mean 'even though'?"

"First of all, Mom, I know what Dad's up to right now, so you don't have to pretend everything's so peachy any more."

Mom carefully draped the afghan over the arm of her chair. She took a deep breath. "Believe me, Vivian. In time we would have discussed it all with you, but there's no need to lose sleep over it. The fact is—we might *all* be better off in the long run."

"Don't you care? Don't you even have a say?"

"Me? A say? Please, Vivian! You know that I'm not crazy about some of your father's antics. There's one thing for sure though, once he decides on something, I don't have the power to change his mind."

"What if you say 'I love you' a hundred times over and throw your arms around him? It's worth a try, isn't it?"

"You read too many Archie comics, Vivian. And now that fantasy garbage you're into! Let me remind you—we're not living in a make-believe world. Just bear this in mind, Vivian, you don't know your father the way *I* do. Once he decides to leave, you can be sure that he'll do just that."

CHESS CLUB "WINNINGS"

There's that noise again. Kchh! Kchh! Kchh! Him. In the kitchen, scraping the burnt edges off his toast. And humming. Same blasted song over and over again. I can't stand the way he just goes about his cheery little life. Doesn't give a hoot about anyone or anything that really matters.

I sat in front of my mirror for a bit, counting up my freckles and trying to see how long I could go without blinking. I figured out that when I see myself in the mirror, I don't even see the *real* me. Like, when I touch my right cheek, my mirror-self touches her left cheek. You don't have to be a scientist to figure this out: While other people can see the *real* me, I only get to see my mirror-me...the one who has her lefts and rights all in reverse.

I yanked the comb through my tangles. My daily tug-o'-war with my hair seemed worse than ever.

Suddenly Dad's reflection appeared in the mirror's doorway. "Vivi. Try combing the ends first," he said.

"Then start combing again, about an inch or two above that, and finally, an inch or two even higher up. You'll see...the tangles will disappear painlessly. Trust me."

I put my comb down. *Oh, man! Why don't you just go back into the kitchen and scratch the edges off your toast! Go hum "Your Cheatin' Heart" for another two or three hours. Just don't bug me!*

His reflection got closer and closer. Before I knew it, Mirror-Dad had picked up my comb and begun working out my tangles. I cringed.

He started to smooth my hair back and then worked it into a loose braid. "How beautiful you are!" he said. "You know, Grandma Rosie's hair was much like yours. I remember when I was a kid. I used to watch her comb her long wavy hair and tie it back with velvet ribbons. Your Grandma—may she rest in peace—she had velvet ribbons in every colour of the rainbow."

How could I hate him so much...and love him so much...all at the same time?

"Got any great plans today, Vivi?"

"No. I'll probably force myself to get some more reading done. I still have that book report hanging over my head. At least they were nice enough to give me an extra week to work on it."

"Aw, darn it. I'm heading over to Hasky's for a few

games of chess and had hoped to invite you along. Boy! Last time, you played so well, you set those old-timers' heads in a spin!"

Great! Now I'm torn between The Hobbit *and the chess club. Torn between going with him and not going with him. If I don't go with him, I'll be bored out of my skull. If I do go with him, I'll get to have a few games of chess with the old-timers.*

"Okay, Dad, I'll go. *The Hobbit* will just have to wait till I get home."

Mom sauntered in, her floppy slippers kerploofing across the floor. "Soon you'll be quite the chess champ, Vivian. It's just too bad Hasky's place stinks like a smoked herring. All those old fogies puffing away on their cheap cigars. Phooey!"

I wasn't thrilled about spending the day with Dad, but I wasn't going to spoil things for myself either.

By nine thirty, we were walking along Saint Urbain Street toward Hasky's. We stopped now and then to check out some of the neighbours' Christmas wreaths along the way.

The weather was especially mild. The icicles clinging to the window ledges and banisters were melting in the sunlight. The water-drops shimmered as they grew, gave up their grip, and plunged into the snow-coated gardens below.

I wanted to ask him stuff, I wanted to tell him stuff,

but I couldn't find the right words. *Suppertime. I promise. That's my absolute deadline. Period. End-of-sentence.*

Hasky's was pretty grungy. Not much of a window display there. Just some old faded cigarette posters behind the smudged up glass.

Dad yanked the door open. The usual blend of smells greeted us. Vanilla. Smoked meat. Mustard. Pipe tobacco.

Mr. Haskell hooked his thumbs into his apron. "Hey, Dan. I see you brought in your sidekick. I'm sure this little pro will soon have the old coots back there shiverin' in their galoshes."

Dad laughed. "She's a keen player, Hasky. Getting better all the time."

Mr. Haskell scrunched up his eyebrows and studied my face. "Say. Aren't you the kid with the toothache?"

I didn't answer. I suppose he read my mind, because he never asked again. *Smart man, Mr. Haskell. You got it all figured out.*

He ran a damp rag over the counter top. "So, what'll it be?" he said. "We just got a batch of spruce beer from this guy Larivière up near Chicoutimi. Bottles it himself. Wanna give it a try?"

"Sure," said Dad. "Make it two."

Mr. Haskell slid two tall glasses onto the counter. I watched the water drops zigzag through the frost on the outside of my glass. Then I took a sip. It tasted like a forest! *Yes-siree. I'll have one of those scrumptious Christmas tree sodas if you don't mind—yuck! I should have ordered a plain old Nesbitt's Orange.*

I forced myself to take a few tiny sips now and then, so Dad wouldn't think he was wasting money on me. While they talked about man-stuff, I swung myself from side to side on the high swivelling stool. I hung onto the counter for dear life, so's not to go flying and wipe out like another Humpty-Dumpty.

Mr. Haskell leaned his elbows on the counter. "Hey, Dan. Did y' catch the game last night? How about that Rocket!"

"Creaming the Black Hawks would'a been enough," said Dad. "But sneaking in his four hundredth goal? That sure was something to see. A real first!"

A man in a long overcoat joined in. "You just wait—they're thirty, these guys, they'll have maybe two teeth left—one on the top right and one on the bottom left. And they won't even be able to chew nothin', let alone stand on skates no more. They'll be all washed up. Who'd want such a life?"

Mr. Haskell sold a couple of newspapers and some pipe tobacco. He tossed the damp rag into the little sink behind him. "Say, fellas. Did y' see the new Buick coming out in the spring? The dealers are starving, y' hear? Soon they're gonna be throwing in rubber mats.

Even radios. Anything to make a sale."

"They could throw in their mother's Auntie Fanny for all I care," said Dad. "My family always sticks with Ford or Studebaker."

Yeah, Studebaker, I said inside. *One every forty years!* My hand bumped along a collection of dried up chewing gum under the counter—*probably stuck there by kids who are now older than Mr. Haskell himself.* Right then I wished I'd brought along some bubble gum.

As if he could read my mind, Dad said, "Vivi, how about a treat from the candy counter?"

Mr. Haskell made his way around the poker players who were huddled at small tables behind the counter. He stopped at the glass showcase. It was jam-packed with gum, blackballs, humbugs and every flavour of Lifesavers.

"What would you like, Vivi?" said Dad.

"I'll go with chocolate-coated raisins, please."

"I would have guessed it," he said. "That's my favourite too, you know." Then he turned to Mr. Haskell. "We'll have two boxes of raisin Glosettes, a pack of Sen-Sen, and a handful of Fleer's Double Bubble."

The short, dark passage leading to the chess club was lined on both sides with dusty wooden cases of Kik. As we entered the back room, I heard a booming voice.

"Hey! Here comes Glayzier with a beautiful lady!"

"Sh-hhhhaaa. Quiet!" roared one of the men from a corner of the room. He turned his pipe upside-down in the ashtray and pounded his knight into place to block another man's king. *"Checkmate!"*

"Well, looks like you got me, Jake," said the man. "Who's next?"

Dad told the man that he was free to play. Jake began to scrape the ashes from the bowl of his pipe. "What about the kid? She plays too?"

"She sure does!" said Dad. "And I warn you, she's a good player."

Jake poked the other man's shoulder. "Tell me, Morris," he said jokingly. "How can such an ugly man have such a beautiful kid?"

Morris laughed. "Yeah. Take a look at them. Just like the beauty and the beast."

All the men at the other tables laughed until they started to cough.

I sat across from Jake, and we set up the board.

Jake made his opening move, then studied my face over the top of his glasses. I was sure he was planning to beat me in three moves. Grandpa had once showed me that trick, and he also taught me how to put a stop to it. I brought my knight forward for the block.

"Gosh, dang!" hollered Jake.

"Hey, watch your language back there," Mr.

Haskell bellowed from the front of the store.

The game continued. Old Jake burped, launching an invisible cloud of sardines and onions across the table.

I knew he'd beat me. He'd taken off my knights, my bishops, one rook and most of my pawns. Finally, he moved his queen right next to my king and called, "Checkmate."

I watched Jake pinch some fresh tobacco from a little black zippered pouch. As he began to stuff it into his pipe, little squiggly bits of tobacco clung to his yellow fingers, then scattered over the chessboard. "Wh-o-o-o's next?" he shouted.

When Dad's game was over, Morris invited me to play at his table.

"You want the white ones?" Morris said.

"Sure. Thank you."

"Most kids like the white pieces," he said. "Ask me...I know."

I moved my king's pawn forward two squares, my usual opening. Morris took lots of time to plan his moves, humming all the while, and tapping his fingers on the edge of the table.

At one point, while all that humming and drumming was going on, I looked up at him. I thought I was seeing things. In his shirt pocket, stuck between his little plastic ruler and a few cheap ballpoints, he had Grandpa's gold fountain pen. Suddenly, I had a terrible sinking feeling and could hardly think about the game any more. All I could think about was Grandpa.

"You like to play chess?" said Morris.

"Yes. Very much."

"Your papa taught you how to play?"

"No, my grandpa."

"Smart man, your grandpa."

"Do you know him?"

"No. Smart for teaching you chess. Maybe, if I was smart, I should teach *my* grandchildren too."

"How many do you have?"

"How many? Such a question! I have more grandchildren than I have fingers on my hands to count them with. Big ones. Little ones. Even one on the way. Sheldon...now he's my oldest. He goes to McGill. A good student. Michael and Shayna are still in high school. Deena's in Grade Six already. The twins started Grade Two this year, and I even have one in kindergarten. The babies? Well...they're still babies. Too young to play chess, eh?"

Holy smokes! This old guy's Deena's grandfather, and he's sporting Grandpa's gold pen right there in his pocket!

"Hello! Hello! You're still playing?"

"I'm sorry. I was thinking about other stuff."

"I can see that. You're mind's not even on the

board. You're a real daydreamer, eh?"

"I...I was actually looking at your gold pen," I said. "Was it a present?"

"Sure! I'll tell you the truth. I never buy a pen. I never buy a cigarette lighter. I never buy a book. I never buy nothin'. Everything I have is a present. A present from *this* one. A present from *that* one. I have more presents than I know what to do with."

I tried to concentrate but got too careless and made some stupid moves. I lost two pawns and a knight. My eyes kept wandering to Morris' shirt pocket. *Now's my only chance. I must get Grandpa's pen back—no matter what.* My fists were scrunched up so tightly, I thought my knuckles would pop right through my skin. What am I supposed to say? *He's gonna think I'm some kind of a lunatic.* "I...I almost telephoned you," I said. "Yesterday I tried over and over to get your number from Deena, but she kept on hanging up on me."

"Why would Deena hang up on you?"

"She's not talking to me any more. Not after yesterday. Know why? Because yesterday I faked losing three dollars at the mountain, and I didn't confess...even after everybody froze to death out there in the snow."

"Sounds like a movie. An Alfred Hitchcock. Anyway, so tell me, why did you almost telephone me?"

"Because when I told Deena that I wanted her to give me the gold pen back, she got mad and said 'forget it...it's too late'. That's why."

Morris looked confused. "Deena has your pen?"

"Not any more. Now *you* have it."

"Little girls talk in such big circles. You're telling me that *my* pen is really *your* pen?"

"No. It's not really mine. It's my Grandpa's."

"Your Grandpa's? Tell me, are we still in the same movie?"

I felt like such a jerk because I couldn't explain it any better. *I'd rather die than have to come right out and beg him for it. I could never do that. But I must! I have to do it. I have to. It's my only hope.* I pointed to his pocket. "I need that gold pen to give to my Grandpa," I said. "I need it very, very badly. As a matter of fact, I need it more than anything in the whole world. My poor Grandpa. He lost his precious pen. The gold pen that was given to him as a present, the last gift that he got from my Grandma. No. He didn't lose it—I took it from him. No. I actually stole it from him and..."

Morris shrugged. "Oy! I don't understand any more. Not one word. But for such a high-falootin' performance, you deserve an Academy Award. I'll tell you what. If you win the game, I'll give you this pen as a prize. You'd like that?"

"Oh, yes. I sure would."

"Good. Then it's a deal."

"But...but what happens if I *lose* the game?"

He looked up at the ceiling and shook his head. "Then...we have a serious problem. But we'll cross that bridge when we come to it."

"How about this?" I said. "If I lose, I'll save up and buy you another pen. Two pens even. Would that be okay?"

He laughed. "Take a good look at me, my little movie-star. Do I look like a man who needs more pens?"

The game continued. I had a great chance to check his king. The best part was that if he moved his king or even blocked it with a pawn, I'd be able to slide my bishop in to take off his rook. And that's exactly how it happened. But my big-shot move backfired. By moving my bishop, I left an opening for his queen to move right in. Ker-plunk. It was checkmate. Game over.

"You play very good chess," said Morris. "You're a fine player."

I stared at Grandpa's pen. "Thank you," I said. "But you're really a whole lot better than I am."

Morris took the pen from his pocket. "Listen. Win...lose... What's the difference? This pen is for you to keep. I have more pens than I have words to write— or paper to write them on."

"Thank you," I gasped. I couldn't believe my luck. While Dad was playing his third game, I went into the storage room and sat down on an empty wooden crate. I unwrapped a Fleer's Double Bubble and began to plan my next move.

"FINDING" GRANDPA'S PEN

It didn't feel at all like December. Even so, I couldn't get away with leaving my hat and gloves at home, because Mom always makes such a big deal about catching colds or ending up with double pneumonia. As we walked along, I could hear the tiny streams trickling between the cracks in the ice underfoot.

"Well," said Dad. "This didn't turn out to be your best day, did it, Vivi?"

"Win...lose... What's the difference, Dad? Either way, I'm glad we went to the chess club today."

"Sorry I spoiled your reading plans. I'll bet you'll be tearing into that book the minute we get home."

"Well, I was actually hoping to drop in on Grandpa today. I'd really like to go pay him a visit, Dad, even for a couple of hours. Can you give me a ride over later? Please?"

"You have your standing visit on Wednesdays. Can it wait till then?"

"I'd rather not wait. Today would be so much better.

C'mon, Dad. I'm sure he wouldn't mind an earlier visit. In fact, this way I'd be able to help him find his pen."

"Good thinking, Vivi. I'll bet he'll be thrilled to see you. Last time I spoke to Grandpa, he sounded so down-in-the-dumps."

When Mom heard our boots clunking up the stairs, she met us at the door. "How'd the games go?"

"I won two and lost one," said Dad, "but Vivi didn't have much luck at all today."

"C'est la vie!" she said. "I'm sure Vivi will win her share next time. Oh, by the way, you got a phone call while you were out."

"I'll just whisk Vivi over to Grandpa's," said Dad. "The call will have to wait till I get back."

Grandpa was looking pretty scruffy. He was wearing one of his faded old shirts and his fix-it-man dungarees. His socks didn't match, and one was even starting to spring a hole at the toe.

"What a surprise!" he said. "How did you know I needed some perking up today?" He straightened the little curtain on the front door and kicked some boots and shoes off to one side so I wouldn't trip over them. "I don't think I could'a made it to Wednesday without seeing my sweet Vivi."

I followed him into the kitchen. He made a poor attempt to clear away some of his junk from the table and went to light up the burner under the whistling kettle.

Grandpa lined up a few empty jars and cans on the table. "C'mon. Y' may as well help me sort out all this junk," he said. "For a start, see if you can match up any of these nuts and bolts. If you get any of 'em matched up, just drop 'em into the bean tin. If you find any that don't match up, put 'em in that soup can over there. Wood screws go into the jam jar, washers in the sardine can. Get it?"

I started to match up the nuts and bolts. "What about these things?"

"Cotter pins, wing nuts, eye-hooks. All those one-of-kind things can get dumped in with the washers. It don't matter much."

When the kettle began to steam, I helped Grandpa carry all the junk into the dining room.

I'm just a few inches away from the holy-mess cabinet. We're talking inches here! I must find a way to get Grandpa's pen out of my pocket and into the cabinet. But how?

Grandpa took the chessboard down from the top of the fridge and opened it up on the kitchen table. We set up our men.

"I played at the club today," I said.

"Did you beat the pants off those old geezers?"

"Oh, Grandpa! I didn't even win one game this time. It really bugs me when I lose."

"Nobody likes losing, Vivi. Why, even the great

champions like Smyslov and Yanofsky get to lose a game now and then. For every winner there has to be a loser, you know. Then, of course, in chess, there's always a chance of a stalemate."

Halfway through the game, the telephone rang and Grandpa got up to answer it.

Now. Do it now. Do it...right...NOW!

I bolted into the dining room and opened the china cabinet as quietly as I could. I was just about to place Grandpa's pen beside the silver bookmark, when he walked into the dining room. Startled, I dropped the pen, and it went skittering across the floor.

"You found it! You found it!" he cried. He clutched the pen and held it close to his heart. "How can I ever thank you, Vivi? This pen is my most treasured gift from Grandma Rosie. You knew that, didn't you?"

In my heart I said, *Oh, yes, Grandpa. Yes. I knew that...but not soon enough. I should never have taken it in the first place, and I'm so glad I got it back for you.*

Grandpa slapped together a couple of tomato and lettuce sandwiches while I peeled and sliced two apples for dessert. Right after lunch we settled back into our game.

"By the way," said Grandpa, "that was your dad on the phone before. He said he had to make an important stop before coming over here, and that your mom was coming along too. Strange, though, he sounded quite agitated."

108

Company's Coming

The sound of the doorbell made me jump right out of my skin. I stayed in the kitchen while Grandpa hurried to the front door. While they were busy kicking their boots off and hanging up their coats, I strained to make out what all the whispering was about, but the wire hangers clanged out their conversation. Dad was first into the kitchen. His look told me that I was in a heap of trouble. Mom followed, along with someone I'd never seen before. Grey hair swept up into a bun. A bit on the chunky side. Glasses with one of those chains attached.

Dad spoke first. His voice shot right through me. "There's no easy way to say this, Vivian. To tell you that I'm disappointed would be far less than accurate. I'm *distressed* by what you've done."

"I'm sorry, Dad. I...I...."

"You certainly have a lot to be sorry about. Why don't you start by apologizing to Miss Villner...for trying to deceive her and for being so disrespectful? After spending most of the weekend agonizing over your nasty phone call, Miss Villner got up the courage to phone me today."

Holy mackerel! That's her? Of all the women in the whole world—that's the one he picks to carry on with. Is he from another planet?

"Well, go ahead, Vivian. I brought Miss Villner here today because you owe her a personal apology. She deserves no less."

I tried to hide my shock. "I'm sorry, Miss Villner. I'm sorry for being so rude to you on the telephone." *How can Mom stand to be in the same room with her?*

"I accept your apology, Victoria."

"Vivian," I said. *Why did I bother correcting her? What difference does it make?*

She folded and unfolded her glasses a few times and looked all flustered and fidgety. "May I ask why you telephoned me, Vivian?"

"I...I called to tell you to stay away from my Dad. It was the only plan I could think of—to stop the divorce."

Dad's eyes nearly popped. "Divorce? What the heck are you talking about?"

"About you and Mom. That's what I'm talking about, Dad. All about how you were screaming at each other and how you said you were leaving. I wasn't in dreamland, you know. Then, when I saw that lady's name and phone number and all that mushy stuff, I knew I had to do something...and I had to do it fast."

Mom was ready to jump in, but Dad interrupted. "You'll have plenty of time to have your say, Jenny, but right now, *I'll* handle this." But for a minute he just stood there with a confused look on his face. "What mushy stuff?"

"I'm not a hundred per cent sure," I said. "But it was about her being so gorgeous or something like that. No. Attractive and tempting. Yes, that's what it was."

He squeezed his eyebrows together like he always does when he thinks real hard. His thinking seemed to go on forever. *Well, I'll be danged!* he burst out. "I didn't write those notes about Miss Villner...although she's a lovely lady indeed. I wrote those comments while I was searching through the employment ads. What was so attractive? Bigger paychecks, Vivian, that's what! And what was so tempting? Finding a job where I wouldn't have that miserable old Henderson hovering over me! I wasn't looking for *trouble*, Vivian. I was looking for a *job.*"

"Oh. But...what...what does that have to do with Miss Villner then?"

"Bernice Villner happens to be the Manager of Metro Work Search...and their most experienced career counsellor to boot."

"I'm still not sure I understand any of this. If there's no divorce, why did you tell Mom that you were leaving?"

He was almost yelling now. *"Leaving?* I never said anything of the sort!"

"You did!" Mom blurted. "Of course you did! Remember, Dan? Just after Vivian went to bed—when was it—Wednesday? In any case, it was the day you were complaining about that good-for-nothing rat, Henderson."

"Yeah, I remember that, Jen, but…"

"That's when you said it, Dan. It was all about your job. You told me you couldn't take it any more—your job, that is—and that you were leaving."

A second after she said that, Mom's mouth dropped open. "Oh, Vivian," she said. "How horrible it must have been for you…to think that we…that we…oh, my goodness!" She hugged me close. "Oh, Vivi, how awful!"

"Well, that's one problem out of the way," said Dad. "I'm sorry to say, though, that we're faced with yet another dilemma. Now, where did Pop disappear to?"

Mom had just poured Grandpa's cold tea down the drain and was rinsing out the granny cup. "He's probably gone into the parlour to get away from all this racket," she said. "You know your Dad better than I do. He's never been able to put up with family squabbles."

Just then Grandpa appeared in the kitchen doorway. "I sure hope all the yellin' is over with," he said. "I'll bet the landlord's enjoyed a good earful."

"Why don't we all go into the parlour," said Dad.

Bernice held back. "Oh my! I hope you don't mind if I wait here in the kitchen. I'd feel like an intruder to sit in on a family discussion...well, one that doesn't involve *me*, that is."

Grandpa dug up a couple of old newspapers from the pile. "Y' may wanna work on a crossword puzzle or two while we're all out there. Might keep y' from gettin' bored."

She smiled. "Why, thank you, er..."

"Walter," he said.

Without a word, we followed Dad into the parlour. Grandpa sat in his favourite armchair near the window. Dad plunked himself onto the chesterfield beside Mom, and I chose the wooden rocking chair beside the bookcase. We sat quietly and waited. Dad stared down at his hands and took a deep breath. "I'd like you to know that the moment I hung up after speaking with Bernice today, the telephone rang. The caller sounded so distraught, I could barely make out what he was trying to say. He told me some things that I found both outrageous and shocking."

MORE COMPANY COMING?

I couldn't imagine what that phone call was all about or why Dad needed to spring it on the whole family. But I was curious just the same. I rocked gently back and forth, happy that my life was completely back to normal. I thanked my lucky stars that I'd gotten Grandpa's pen back and that the divorce thing was all a big mistake.

Dad walked over to Grandpa and leaned on the arm of his chair. "I'm awfully sorry, Pop. I never meant to trigger such a big showdown here today."

Grandpa laughed. "Well, I s'pose we gave the landlord enough dirt to fill up a bestseller."

"About that phone call, Pop, the one I just mentioned, I hope you don't mind that I asked the fella to drop by here this afternoon. He said it was most important that he see me, and the sooner the better."

"Heaven help us!" said Grandpa. "I could have enjoyed a nice relaxing Sunday afternoon, but NO!

My son here has taken the liberty of inviting a whole houseful of guests."

The man at the door looked even older than Grandpa. His hair was perfectly white, and he had a great big walrus moustache that hung down on both sides, halfway down to his chin. The man stuffed his gloves into his coat pockets and shook hands with Dad. "My name's Maxwell Nagelvasser," he said. "But you can call me Max. Just plain Max."

"C'mon into the parlour," said Dad. "Pop, this is Max, the gentleman who telephoned me earlier today. I'd like you to meet my father, Walter. This is my wife, Jenny and my daughter, Vivian." Grandpa looked curiously at the stranger in his parlour. They shook hands.

"I'm sorry to barge in on you and your family like this, but I have to clear something up, and I don't think it can wait an extra minute."

Mom scooped up a pile of *National Geographic*s from one of the bridge chairs. "Please sit down," she said.

"I'm not myself today," said Max. "So please bear with me. I just had a big falling-out with one of my grandchildren, and getting information out of her was like getting blood from a rock! Here's what happened. A couple of nights ago, she gave me a gold fountain pen, the nicest birthday present I ever got. This morning, my daughter, who knows about these things, came to visit me. She took a good look at my present. 'This is no cheap pen,' she said. 'Even with the generous allowance Deena gets, she could never afford to buy such a gift'."

I couldn't hold back for another second. "But you're not Deena's grandfather," I said. "Her grandfather is Morris."

He looked confused. "Morris?"

"Let the gentleman finish, Vivian," said Mom. "It's was very rude of you to interrupt."

What the heck's he trying to pull here? He's not Deena's grandfather. Morris is. He said so himself. What kind of no-good stunt is this guy up to?

Max pulled a gold pen from inside his jacket. "So I ask my granddaughter, 'Where did you get this pen?' And she answers, 'I bought it from somebody.' So I say, 'Who did you buy it from? Who?' She hems and haws a bit, then tells me, 'A kid in school.' 'What kid?' I say, 'Does he have a name?' It was like pulling, teeth, I tell ya. Then she finally says, 'Vivian. Vivian Glayzier.'"

Holy Jeepers! Who was Morris, then?

Grandpa rushed into the dining room. He came back with the gold pen—the one Morris had given me in the chess club. He pulled the curtains open and studied the pen carefully in the sunlight. He turned it this way and that, slowly twisting it between his thumb and fingers. "Vivian!" he roared. "What kind of low-down trickery are you into? What have you done?"

"I...I thought it was yours, Grandpa. I really thought it was your pen."

"Well, it's not! How did this thing get into my cabinet?"

The truth, Vivian. The truth. The truth. "I got it off this guy Morris at the chess club," I said. "He told me it would be a prize for winning the game, but even though I lost, he still wanted me to have it. I was sure that Morris was Deena's grandfather. I thought so because he even said that his granddaughter's name was Deena and that he got the pen as a present. I was sure it was your pen, and I was so glad to get it back for you."

"Get it *back* for me? What the heck's that supposed to mean?"

"I'm sorry, Grandpa. Please don't hate me."

"Who's this Deena to you? How did she get my pen in the first place?"

"I...I sold it to her. I took it right out of your china cabinet. I'm sorry, Grandpa. I sold it to Deena because I needed some money real bad."

He threw his hands up into the air. "That's stealing, darn it! You stole my pen!" he shouted. "How dare you do such a thing!"

My words were locked inside. I wanted to crumble up. Be invisible. Having Grandpa scream at me like that was like having the heart ripped right out of me.

Deena's grandfather struggled with his boot buckles, then did up his overcoat. "Sorry I caused so much trouble here today," he said.

"Trouble? Never!" said Grandpa. "You have no idea what this pen means to me. I can't thank you enough."

After Deena's grandfather left, Mom and Dad joined Bernice in the kitchen. She'd finished two crossword puzzles and was almost falling asleep working on her third.

Mom tapped Bernice gently on her shoulder. "We'd better get you home," she said softly. "I feel so awful for having put you through a day like this."

"I admit, I was a tad uncomfortable," said Bernice, "but there's really no need to apologize, Jenny. I understand."

"Believe me," said Mom. "I told Dan it was most inappropriate to drag you here today. I told him it would have been better to bring Vivian to your office after school tomorrow. But he was so upset, there was no reasoning with him."

"You're right, Jenny," said Dad. "I made a hasty decision, and I'm very sorry. C'mon, Bernice. Jenny and I will drive you home right away. And as for you, Vivian, we'll drop by for you later. I'm sure you and Grandpa need to spend some time together right now. Alone."

CLEANING SOLUTION

Look how he just sits and stares out the window like that. He probably can't stand the sight of me. He hates me. Hates me. I know it. He'll probably never speak to me again.

Grandpa slowly turned from the window. He combed his fingers through his silvery hair. "I'm surprised at you!" he said. "A young lady of eleven should know better."

My face was hot with shame, and my eyes started to fill up with tears. "I know it's not enough to just say 'I'm sorry,' Grandpa, but I am. I'm very sorry for what I've done."

Grandpa nudged the edge of the chessboard to line it up with the tabletop. "Well, there's no sense in staring off into space," he muttered and slowly advanced one of his pawns. "It's your move," he said. His voice was like ice. He traced his finger around the rim of the granny-cup. *"Rats!"*

"Rats?"

"Yeah. You heard right. Big-fat-stinkin'-garbage-pickin'-rats!"

"I know you hate me now. You do, don't you, Grandpa?"

"No. I could never hate you, Vivian. I'm just shocked at what you've..."

"I wish I could erase it. I wish I could wind the clock backwards and start all over again from Wednesday. Everything would be so different."

He lowered his head and almost whispered, "What's done...is done. There's nothing we can do about it."

We slipped back into silence, fixing our eyes on anything but each other. I checked out Grandpa's collection of old newspapers and magazines stacked along the wall, the mountain of dishes and pots piled high beside the sink, and the grease-stained oven door. "I've got it! I've got it, Grandpa! How about this? I'll help you clean up around here. I'll shine up the whole kitchen. I'll dust all your bookshelves and help you tidy up all your..."

"Whoa! Just hold it right there! I'd never ask you to do anything of the sort—and you know it. The last thing in the world I need is for *you* to be my charlady, for heaven's sake!"

"You wouldn't have to *ask* me, Grandpa. I want to do it. I really want to."

Grandpa leaned back in his chair. "Look," he said, "I get what you're trying to say, Vivian. I'll be the first to admit it, I'm king of the slobs. Truth is, I'm ashamed when company drops in—like today. This place is a bloody mess, isn't it?"

"Will you let me, then? Please?"

He reached across the table and took my hand. "Your idea is brilliant!" he said. "But before we even consider it, answer me this...you say the whole thing started because you needed some money real bad. Is that right?"

"Yes, Grandpa. I don't get very much allowance, you know, and sometimes, by Friday, I don't even have two pennies to scrape together...or something like that. You know what I mean."

"Very well then. When you drop in on Wednesday evenings, you can spend the first part of your visit playing 'cleaning lady'. Of course, to my way of thinkin', that's worth about two bucks an hour."

"But, Grandpa..."

"No buts, Vivian. You've come up with quite a plan...and if we can swing a deal here, we'll *both* be better off."

THE DIARY—
TURNING A NEW LEAF

Friday, April 1, 1955

Dear brand new 1955 sky blue diary with silver all around the edges—

This is not an April Fools' joke! Mom and Dad actually bought me a new diary for my 12th birthday! Way back in December, on the night of the big kerfuffle at Grandpa's, I tore the first few pages out of my old diary and stashed them away in a drawer. Then I threw my diary into the coal-stove. As it hit the hot coals, the sparks danced and crackled all around it. Before long, the flames licked the gold paint away from the edges and twisted the pages all out of shape. I watched the fire destroy my precious diary...and leave nothing in its place but ashes. I don't think I'll ever forget the choking smell of plastic, melting and sizzling on the hot coals. Mom and Dad told me that they were proud of me for doing that.

Over the last few months, aside from saving up

the five dollars to give back to Deena, I was able to put away enough money for some stuff I needed down on Main Street.

So, now my life's <u>really</u> back to normal. Maybe better than normal. I haven't had to visit The Elephant since the day I telephoned Bernice. Of course, I did go in one day to tell him that I was all wrong about the divorce.

A lot's happened since my diary went up in flames. Shelly and I are best friends now. She loves to come over to listen to records, play Scrabble, or just shoot the breeze for a while.

Deena has a new bunch of friends again. Whenever she gets into name-calling or starts getting too bossy, her friends just vamoose. It's so much easier not trying to be <u>her</u> best friend any more.

Dad's been in his new job for over two months now, thanks to Bernice. This morning he promised he'd go with Mom to check out a couple of street-level flats that are up for rent. I heard Mom say, "It'll be so much easier if we move into a bottom flat— now that the family tree's sprouting a new branch." That's her way of saying "you-know-what."

– Vivian

THE GIFT

I never thought of Wednesday as being my favourite day, but yesterday was a whole lot different. Don't get me wrong. I didn't suddenly wake up in the morning looking forward to a history lesson. Nothing like that. Through every class, I caught myself daydreaming about my visit to Grandpa's. I was so excited about delivering his gift and tried to imagine the look on his face when he unwrapped it.

The whole day seemed to drag along much too slowly for me. First school, then homework, then suppertime.

At last! Dad dropped me off at seven thirty. The minute Grandpa opened the door, I knew something was strange. He wasn't dressed in his fix-it-man dungarees. He was wearing a new sport shirt and a pair of snazzy corduroys. He had no sign of five-o'clock shadow, and his shoes were freshly polished.

I sniffed the air. "What's that stuff you got on, Grandpa?"

"Oh, just a little splash of Old Spice," he said. "Like it?"

"Sure," I said. "Smells a bit like cinnamon, doesn't it?"

"Oh, I don't think so, Vivi. This stuff has a smell all its own. The cinnamon's from the pie."

"Pie? Since when do *you* know how to bake a pie?"

"I guess there's still a few things about me you don't know, Vivi."

I leaned Grandpa's gift against the wall in the dining room. "Did you use one of Grandma's recipes?"

He shook his head. "Nope."

"Aha! You picked it up at Steinberg's then, right?"

Just then, I heard something clanging around in the kitchen. "What was that?"

"Company," said Grandpa. "I've got company."

"Did you say you've got company?" called a voice from the kitchen.

"Sure thing!" said Grandpa. "C'mon out here."

Holy smokes! Am I seeing right?

Bernice carried a tray into the dining room and set it down on the table. One glorious apple pie! One little brown teapot. One chipped mug. One granny-cup. "Vivian. How nice to see you!" she said. Her voice was warm and friendly.

"Now, see here," said Grandpa. He reached for Bernice's

hand. "I s'pose it's time you knew, Vivi, that Bernice and I have become sorta...well...how can I put it?"

"Romantic?"

"That's it!" he said. "That's the word I was lookin' for. When I saw this lovely lady tear into a crossword puzzle with a ballpoint pen, I knew she was my kinda girl."

"Does that mean you're...going steady?"

Grandpa blushed. I'd never seen him blush before.

Bernice twisted the corner of her apron. "Would you like a cup of tea, Vivian?"

"No, thank you," I said. "I'm more into hot chocolate."

"I'll be happy to make you one," she said. "I only hope I remember how."

Bernice brought a cup of hot chocolate into the dining room. It was almost perfect. It just needed a bit more milk to get it to the right shade.

As Bernice cut the apple pie into wedges, I placed Grandpa's gift on the dining room table in front of him. "This is for you, Grandpa."

"For me? In April?"

"It's not a birthday present. It's just a plain ol' present. I wanted to do something extra-special for you."

"But you already have. You've turned this dump into a palace, Vivi."

"No fair counting that, Grandpa. Things you get

paid for don't really count as extra-special, you know."

He began to untie the ribbon. "Well, then...I'd better unwrap it before y' change your mind."

"Don't worry, Grandpa. There's no chance of that."

The gift wrap fell to the floor.

"A new chessboard!" he cried. "This is just what I needed." His smile faded to a frown. "Gads! I hope this didn't set y' back a big bundle of cash."

"Not at all," I said. "I got all the stuff at Tremblay Hardware. The wood, the tiles, cement...everything."

His eyebrows flew up. "You made this?"

"Oh, yes. The old board was looking kind of flimsy and fall-apart...so I made you a new one."

"It's incredible! How did you get it so perfect?"

"Oh, Grandpa! I did exactly what you told me. I spent most of my time planning and measuring. The rest was as easy as pie."

"Speaking of pie," said Bernice. "Would you like a big scoop of ice cream on yours, Vivian?"

Grandpa slowly drew his fingers over the shiny tiles of his new chessboard. He pushed his chair back and stood up, never taking his eyes away from mine. Then he gave me a gigantic hug. A hug that lifted me right off the floor and swung me around in a circle. "You're ready for life," he said. "My precious Vivian, you're ready for life."

Sarah Hartt-Snowbell grew up in Montreal, the setting for *Vivian Untangled*. She admits that, although she started out as a school-phobic non-reader, she now believes that children should be given an early introduction to reading—to establish and reinforce a lasting comfort with books.

Sarah's first published story is a picture book, *A Little Something* (Napoleon, 1998). Her second, *Yesterday's Santa and the Chanukah Miracle* (Napoleon, 2002), was turned into an animated cartoon by the CBC.

Now retired, Sarah dabbles in many hobbies, including word-games, entertaining, ten-pin bowling and painting. Sarah lives in Toronto with her husband. She has two grown children and five grandchildren.